HAN M GREENBARG

Vow Of The Silent Kindred

Contents

One

Marnie

Tuesday, September 12th, 2056. 3:25 PM

Tell me if I'm wrong. We all think we're the masters of life. We think we know how the game is played and how to get what we want through a variety of spontaneous and maybe not-so-wise ways. But it's bigger than that, isn't it? This journey through the world is beyond anything we can really understand.

<u>Paper Airplane Message from Eldon:</u> **Hey, baby. Feel like taking a break? We can grab a mocha and walk the trail. Maybe dance around the trees like you used to do.**

Seriously. Life has changed. But it's been the best adventure. More than I ever could have imagined. I write my response and work on forming my own paper airplane, glancing up to see his cute smile as I prepare to make it fly.

I can't believe it's been this long since Eldon and I first met. We had no idea how our worlds would change. And neither of us could have predicted the outcome of that dreamlike college class encounter. Things happen for a reason. I've always known that. But sometimes it's easy to forget the magic of true adventure and love.

it's easy to forget the magic of true adventure and love.

Two

Eldon

Monday, September 17th, 2012. 9:25 AM. San Luis Obispo, CA

Text From Geoff: BRO U SEE THE GIRLS THIS SEMESTER? NO JOKE. WAY HOTTER THAN LAST YEAR. GRAB A BEER WITH ME AND MARK TONIGHT AFTR CLSSES. I'LL PICK A DATE FR YOU.

I had a weird feeling in my gut the whole night before which my roommates proclaimed to be from their gift of soggy nachos and leftover pizza. I rarely ate the food they brought into the apartment so it was plausible. *Then again...everything that Geoff brings into the apartment upsets my mind and stomach. I don't know why I stick around him. He's dumb, crass trouble in walking form.*

"Hi, El. Same class again, huh?"

I barely nodded at the girl talking to me. She and I, and I always forgot her name, kept having classes together. Calling it annoying was a vast understatement.

"What are the odds?" she said.

Exactly. I put my head down and went back to writing in my binder. *What, indeed, are the odds, Miss Sunflowery Sassdancer?*

Three

Marnie

9:35 AM

Text From Tawny: SRRY, MARN. GOT CAUGHT UP IN GRP MEETNG. TELL ME ABT THAT SCIENCY GUY 2MRW, K? DONT FALL ASLEEP IN MS MONOTONE'S CLASS. LOL

I've always had a love-hate relationship with my own kind. I mean it was never as fun hanging out with girls because they were always trying to compete for attention and nothing was ever chill. I really thought that life would get easier after high school but I was wrong.

Every guy could be the one. Mr. Right Future Husband must be hibernating.

The battle to talk to guys was the worst. I couldn't get close to a cute guy without being literally pushed aside by the more fashionable and loud girls. But I guess I did it to myself though with the whole Elf princess outfit.

I was annoyed for two reasons as I walked into class. Number One: Being late was my least favorite thing. And Number Two: I immediately noticed four girls dressed like it was one hundred degree melt-your-clothes-off weather when it was amazingly breezy outside. I looked for an empty seat, preferably in a corner, and then suddenly: *Who is that?*

Been on this campus for three years and I've only just now seen a guy dressed like this? Not the whole fantasy costume, but he has the pointy ears, long blond hair, and even pirate-like gold earrings?! He looks drop dead gorgeous while sitting there. And the empty chair next to him. YES. That's so mine.

Four

Eldon

9:42 AM

I briefly glanced up to see who just sat to the left of me. *Be still my imaginative Elf heart. It's a princess. She has pointy ears too.* I tried not to look at her as she stared at me. *How did this happen? Two people obsessed with dressing like Elves meeting in the same room? Why haven't I seen her before? Is she a transfer?*

Oooh that gorgeous red hair. She just smiled at me. Darn it. She looks too amazing to not have a boyfriend. Wonder how I can ask this... I don't want her to move away because I'm not smiling back. But she doesn't know I just don't like smiling very much. Oh! I'll try a page from Geoff's Brass Nuts And Bolts Dating Guide: **Rule 4. Girls think passing notes is romantic in this era of overbearing technology.**

I wrote down on a piece of paper in my binder: **Hi. Just a random, friendly curiosity, do you have a boyfriend?**

She didn't answer when I showed it to her, probably because class had started and she didn't want to get in trouble. But then she wrote in blue ink beneath it: **No. I'm single. You?**

Wow. So confident. Concise. And that look in her eyes. **Single,** I wrote.

She smiled before opening her laptop and paying attention to the blah-blah-blahs of the professor up front. I returned to working on my story, writing a line of dialogue next to my terrible sketch of Jaeger Bowen.

"Hey," she whispered, pointing with a pen. "Who's that?"

I decided to speak instead of write, although I was told by my family that I sucked at whispering. They said I mumbled too much. "Jaeger Bowen," I said.

"He's an Elf?"

"He's an elvish superhero from the future. Got stuck in a mission aiding the artisans of Earth."

"Why do artisans need aid?"

So cute. She's really into this. Must be one of those geeky girls who appreciates backstories.

"Because modern society is trying to destroy pure art with robots. Jaeger Bowen has to lead the charge to shut down all the AI systems."

"When's that destruction supposed to happen?" she asked.

"Oh, it's in here," I said, tapping my binder. "First draft of my book. I'm a superhero novelist." *This is awesome. I'm talking with a girl about odd, specific stuff. And she's not rolling her eyes or moving away.*

Five

Marnie

10:25 AM

I braced myself every time the professor looked in our direction. But she seemed to just really enjoy her own voice and didn't care that we were barely taking notes. I learned the art of faking note-taking in eighth grade and by tenth grade I was a master at it.

The Elf prince seemed more nervous than I was, and the more he explained Jaeger Bowen, the more his blue eyes widened. *So adorable... I can't believe I'm sitting next to such a cute, sexy guy. What are the odds?*

"All right, stop the chatter!" the prof finally called out. "Turn your attention to the video."

But even after the lights were dimmed in the classroom, I found myself itching to say one more thing to the Elf prince. I had my laptop open instead of a notebook, so I reached over and scribbled on his binder page: **I'm Marnie.**

Without hesitation, he wrote: **I'm Eldon.**

Eldon. I felt my face get hot and swished my hair to hide my eyes. *Okay, okay. I'm good. I'm not getting my hopes up. I'm totally calm. Why* do I feel like I'm sixteen again? I'm gonna do something stupid I just know it. And so many other girls on campus who must want him. Crap.

Six

Eldon

10:52 AM

Marnie, I thought. *What a name. Fitting for such a gorgeous princess.*

That was the fastest hour of class ever, and with the consistent stares that we gave each other, it was the most enjoyable hour of my life too. I took my time gathering up my backpack and headed out of the building, noticing Marnie following close behind. My plan had been to go straight to the cafeteria to grab a snack and write more before the next class, but seeing how I was being stalked by a cute girl, I didn't really want to pass up the opportunity to see how far she would take it.

This is like a magical quest with Marnie being the adventurer and me being the cool, shiny object of power at the end. I've never felt this awesome.

I changed course, stopping briefly to lean against the campus bookstore and scribble in my binder. Right when I stopped, Marnie stopped. She took out her phone and pretended to text. *The difference between real and pretend texting is obvious: No one bites their lip and falters that much in hand movement. Especially girls. They text so fast it's a blur of nails...unless they're texting an imaginary recipient.*

I hated admitting to myself that I was falling hard for a stranger. That maybe I was being completely illogical and unreasonable in my hope that we would become a real thing down the line. I had never had success with girls beyond the initial ogling and surface talk. Something about my eccentric mannerisms and social awkwardness sent them racing back to their cultured circles. And then they would tell all their friends about the strange Elf-obsessed guy that didn't belong in modern society.

Look at her. Weaving between trees to keep up with me and now she's mumbling to herself while tying her shoe next to the fountain. I haven't seen this sort of epically goofball behavior from a college girl. It's like she knows exactly how to make me laugh. Where in the name of fae and goblins did she come from? Is it just another cruel illusion to crush the old soul romantic within me?

Seven

Marnie

11:30 AM

I wasn't stalking him exactly, but I knew he might think that. At one point he disappeared into the cafeteria. That was where I stopped. *Should I? I don't like being in the cafeteria. It's too claustrophobic. Someone always steals the one table by the left corner that I like. And then, of course, I feel awkward waiting in line with the hope that there will be one more marshmallow brownie in my reach. There never is. Why do I end up in the same line as everyone else who's craving brownies?*

Text From Tawny: HOWD CLSS GO? WHO FELL ASLEEP? HAHA. WAS MELISSA THERE AGAIN SHOWING OFF TO THE GUYS?

I groaned. *Melissa. The one girl on campus who I resented more than any other. I called her "the Forbidden Siren". She just had to wear the shortest skirts and the croppiest tops and they were always brightly colored to match her neon lipstick and magazine-cover-smooth chocolate brown hair. AND she's in the same art class with me and Eldon. Hello, competition. Really. Why does college have to be harder than high school?*

Text To Tawny: DONT SAY THT SIRENS NAME. *Seriously, girl.*

Don't.

Not thinking clearly, I walked right into the cafeteria, eyes still looking at my phone. And then I glanced up to see if the table that I liked was free.

Eldon.

Eldon was sitting there. He was sitting at the table that I never got, and smartly, his backpack was on the other chair so that no one could sit near him. *Cool. Couldn't have timed this better today. I want to talk more with him. How do I approach? Okay, I can do what I've done in the past and see if he glares or turns his back. I'm good at asking really awkward questions. Guys always think I'm a funky piece of work.*

I took a breath and walked over. "Eldon, this will be a stupid question, but why are you single?"

"Because I'm annoying," he said.

No way, Eldon. You're the hottest, cutest, geekiest guy I've met. "So am I. All the guys who are interested in me think they found a winner until I open my mouth and start talking."

"Well," he said, as if my approaching him without an invite was totally normal, "I got you beat in quirks and strange traits."

"Doubt it," I said.

"Okay then. You first." He gestured with a fry, strands of hair falling over his eyes like a sexy warrior. "List 'em."

I grinned when he moved his backpack off the other chair. "Deep-minded introvert with an old soul," I said, sitting down.

"Same." He casually lifted his hand for a high-five. I acknowledged. "What else?" he asked.

"I'm always lost in my story worlds."

"Same." He offered me another high-five.

"I cry easily at every movie I watch," I said. "People think I'm being too dramatic but I dispense happy and sad tears at the drop of a hat."

"I like to say idioms wrong on purpose," he said.

The fact that he remained expressionless while talking was very funny to me. He had a dry, blunt way of existing… and it was eccentric and charming.

"I like black coffee more than sugary ones," I said.

"I'm a picky eater."

We went back and forth, the conversation firing off butterflies like fireworks through my stomach. I felt like I was in a dream.

"I want a lake cabin with a ton of acreage and six dogs in the mountains," I said.

"I have dentures," he said, taking another bite of vanilla pudding.

Dentures, I thought. *Why is that cute to me?* "People think I'm pretentious because I have high standards," I said.

"Same. I don't judge anyone. Just trying to live life the way I believe."

"Do you know how strange it is that we're still talking to each other?"

"Yeah," he said. "Especially since I told you about my dentures. You didn't even flinch."

"Do you really?"

"Just top," he said. "Partials."

There was a brief silence between us and I grinned.

"What?"

"Nothing. You just look so much like Legolas."

He half-smiled and looked down at his pudding cup.

"I'm afraid of fire," I said.

"I'm afraid of thunder."

"I've never had a guy tolerate my randomness for so long."

"Yeah." He slid the cup to the left and folded his arms on the table, looking directly into my eyes. "I hear that. No other girl has stuck around this long for a conversation. All my conversations get really bizarre."

He hasn't walked away. He talks about weird, random things too. It's like the whole crazy soulmate thing might actually be legit.

"Marnie, do you ever pretend you're on a real roller coaster during that intro in the movie theater?"

"Yeah. I get goosebumps every time."

"Me too." We traded high-fives.

"Do the people in the theater look at you like you've completely lost your marbles?"

"Yes."

"I would've said 'lost your sticks' but not sure if I should drop in my deliberately wrong idiom."

"No, I like it. It's funny."

"You're the first," he said. "You're pretty cool, Marnie."

"Thanks, but I'm always the weird one writing crazy stories in the back of class."

"There's nothing weird about that. I do it too."

"Yeah."

"I love that I'm not the only one in an art class writing a story instead of taking proper notes. And my doodles are nothing like the real artists sitting with us in there."

This whole semester we get to be in Art History together. Unreal. I looked at my phone and saw the time. "Shoot. Gotta get to my next class."

"Yeah?" Eldon stood up with me. "What is it?"

"Astronomy."

"Me too!" He grinned wide, showing his teeth for the first time, and his voice was suddenly as loud as a hyped-up-on-sugar boy cheering for his favorite superhero. "I'm glad I know someone before going into a new classroom."

"Social anxiety?" I said.

"Yeah. A little. You'd think after years of school I'd be used to it but I really hate walking into unknown territory."

Unknown territory. Yeah. Wearing prosthetic Elf ears in a modern fast-paced society. For sure we are both eccentric in that aspect. "Me too."

"That's why I dress like my character Jaeger Bowen." He grinned again as we walked, and I held my breath when his arm brushed against mine. *This guy likes talking to me. He's looking at me with a heartthrob's intensity.* "What do you think, Marnie? Does this coat work with my hair?"

"It's more steampunk than fantasy, isn't it? Your coat?"

"Yeah." He looked down at himself. "I guess this is more steampunk-looking."

"And your hair is cool," I said. "Elf warrior and pirate in one."

"Thanks. I'm definitely going for the Elf look."

"Then is your story a mix of steampunk and fantasy?"

"It is a mix. Set in multiple worlds. Of course, I get to bend the rules when it comes to logic in the telling. Jaeger Bowen isn't a rational being."

"He isn't?"

"No. He's highly emotional." In his excitement of explaining it to me, Eldon had a bit of a lisp in his speech. *So adorable.* We strolled across campus together, the sea breeze rippling through our coats. He was wearing the most theatrical floor-length navy blue coat…elegant high collar and buttons…and he let it fly behind him like a cape. *I'm just losing track of what he's saying as I gaze at his awesomeness.* "Adapting to the coldness of Earth is tough for his heart. And yet he lives among the humans as if he was part of their kind. He has to save the artisans."

I could sense Eldon getting emotional as he talked. It was not his character Jaeger he was referring to. It was himself. The exact same way I talked about my story character Arrowswan. I used her as my weapon and voice on Earth. Neither of us felt like we belonged in the modern world, but we were.

"So, when are you scheduled to graduate?" I asked him.

"Next spring. You?"

"Me too. What's your major?"

"English. Not to teach it or anything. Ideally I'll be writing stellar screenplays in the future."

"That's awesome," I said. "Mine is Communication Studies. Had to pick something to major in but I really just want to write novels. I've already published one collection of novellas online, and I've written and published four children's books that my sister illustrated."

"Cool." Eldon and I lingered in the open door, looking at each other before going into class. "I'd love to read your writing, Marnie."

I blushed and almost giggled. *Don't act like a tween, Marn. You're twenty-two for goodness sakes. It's not like he's Legolas in real life.* A guy saying he would love to read my writing while he actually looked like a proper Elf…that was a dream come true.

"Oh, by the way, I do have a very specific question," he said.

"Yeah?"

"Who were you texting when you were following me?"

Oh…nuggets. I plopped into the first empty seat I saw.

"Seriously," Eldon said. He smirked as he sat beside me, pushing his long hair behind his ears.

I couldn't answer while watching him tie his hair back. *Why does he have to drive me crazy like this? Does he know how epic he looks? Break out the archery and wild horses, people. If only we could be under a waterfall with his hair getting all wet and him holding me in the tightest embrace. He smells like a magical forest.*

"Daydreaming, huh?" he said. "I do that all the time. My family could never stand it when I lived in their house."

"Myself," I blurted.

"What?"

"I was texting myself. Gotta be honest, right?"

"Agreed." His mouth was serious and his eyes were laughing. "That's a great tactic."

Eight

Eldon

12:25 PM

I thought that Marnie might be dressed like a character from a real movie or TV show, and I wanted to be certain of that before directly asking if she was an Elf of her own creation.

"I told you about Jaeger Bowen," I said. "What about you? Do you have a made-up character that you like to portray?"

Marnie grinned after glancing at the loud group of collegians coming in behind us. "Arrowswan." She made a sweeping motion to herself, lightly tapping the tiara pinned to her hair and the cloak draped around her shoulders. "She's my Elf self. And I'm writing an epic novel about her adventures using her name as the title."

Marnie's eyes. Her eyes are lingering on mine. Shoot. Don't lose your train of thought, boyo. "Arrowswan," I said aloud, frustrated at my struggle to get the "s" sounds out without faltering. My anxiety was rocketing up the longer we stared into each other's souls.

"Yeah. I thought of it two years ago when I was walking on the beach.

I picked up a kite that someone had lost, saw that it had a swan on it, and I don't know why but the oddball writer in me put that image and the image of an Elf doing archery together and yeah." Marnie shrugged as she started typing. "The name Arrowswan just came to my head."

I held back a smile as I turned to a fresh sheet of paper in my binder. Marnie fearlessly said whatever was in her mind. And so attractive to me, in fact, that I had to shut down naughty thoughts in my head a million times over. *What is it about this angel that's sending me off a cliff?*

The professor was ten minutes into giving his introduction when I realized someone had pushed their bag into the back of my head and was now plunking down on the other side of me. I knew immediately, without looking, who it was. That same annoying girl who kept ending up in my classes and had to announce it all the time. Miss Sunflowery Sassdancer.

"Hey, El. What are the odds?"

I didn't fake a smile. I looked at Marnie whose head was low behind her laptop, sensing that she also held some terrible grudge against the too-sunshiney-sassy-flashy girl.

All right, Eldon, I thought. *You can win good guy points right here if you play this scene out carefully. Geoff's Brass Nuts And Bolts Dating Guide:* **Rule 7. To stop an annoying girl's conversing or advances, make up a totally out-of-context, out-of-nowhere excuse. She will most likely give you a sour, pouty-lipped face or cuss in a snarly voice. Remember to not take offense since you were the one who initiated the unpleasant transaction.**

I had never been bold enough to try that one. But meeting Marnie changed my thought process. She changed a lot of things.

Nine

Marnie

12:32 PM

I honestly thought I was about to lose Eldon right there and then. With my luck, it seemed that I wasn't meant to have such a sweet, sexy guy as my own friend. *The Forbidden Siren wins another one. Darn freakin nuggets.*

I considered moving to a different seat just to avoid further heartache and jealousy, but I heard Eldon say to her: "Would you mind sitting over there?"

"What?" Her hair flipped hard over her shoulder as she looked at him. Her voice was whiny.

"My doctor says I can't be near yellow shirts. I'm allergic."

"Allergic to yellow shirts?"

"No. Allergic to yellow," Eldon said. He was deadpan in his delivery. My favorite kind of humor. He may as well have been standing on stage at a sold out comedy show. "I have a sun allergy and that counts as the sun," he said calmly. "It's way too bright. Could you maybe just scoot down?"

Oh my gosh. I thought about faking a cough, doing my best not to bust into uproarious laughter. I hadn't wanted to laugh that hard in school since the first year on campus when I watched a fellow collegian slip on an uncracked walnut and windmill his arms in every direction for two minutes straight while he tried not to fall.

"I'm not scooting down." The Forbidden Siren snapped her gum and continued pulling junk out of her five hundred dollar purse.

Eldon tilted his head, shrugged dramatically, and turned to me. "Sorry," he whispered loudly. Multiple people could hear him. "I tried, Arrowswan. Couldn't get the goblin princess to exit our kingdom."

It was silent in the room except for my muffled laughter. I knew that Eldon knew he had charmed me because he flashed the largest heart-throbbing, dimple-revealing grin before clicking a green ink pen and writing in his binder.

That hour of class was wasted in my daydreaming mode. All I could do was sneak looks at him, thinking about the ridiculous and hilarious line he delivered to the Forbidden Siren.

Ten

Eldon

1:40 PM

Marnie's laugh was contagious. She was the best audience I'd had for my unintentionally comedic moments, and really, she was so beautiful in her fits of giggles. I couldn't stop smiling as we walked toward the center pavilion on campus, and I hoped that Marnie would continue to lose it the whole way.

"It doesn't take much to get you going, does it?" I said.

She took a breath, stopping to fix the clasp of her silver cloak. "Yeah, I love random things. I don't always know what will crack me up but if I'm in the right mood I'll be a mess about the same joke for hours at a time."

Cute, I thought. *I want to make her laugh more.*

"Hey, Marnie!"

Marnie and I saw an excited, blue-haired girl wildly waving her arms in the middle of the pavilion, and I wondered if this was a rival or a friend.

"Tawny!" Marnie called back. "I thought you said you couldn't meet up until tomorrow."

Okay, I thought. *Marnie looks happy to see her. Must be a friend.*

"Well," Tawny said, gesturing to a couple other girls behind her, "these two said they saw videos of your dancing and I told them you're here on campus. They wanna see that you can actually move like that."

Wait. I halted as Marnie approached her friend. *This adorable beauty can dance?*

"You dance?" I asked. "Do you take classes?"

Marnie answered while tossing her cloak onto a bench. "Nah, it's just for fun. Self-taught."

I planned to give a polite greeting to the other girls, but before I said anything to them, a blast of music drew our attention to the sidewalk.

"Show it off, Marn!" a black-haired jock in red jogging pants said as he held up his phone.

Of all the songs she could dance like a rhythmic spitfire to, it was "Blue" by Eiffel 65. And Marnie did indeed show off.

HOT. Touch-the-sun HOT. Oh baby. I never saw shuffle dancing in person before, but seeing Marnie do it with the speed and precision that she did…and her leading the way when several other collegians jumped in. *Cue spine chills. Omg. Marnie. Baby.*

"Darn it," I whispered to myself.

I had zero rhythm, zero athletic ability. Three sporty dudes were dancing real close to Marnie's butt, and I just wanted to punch them so that I could scoop her up and lean her against the hood of a black Lamborghini (that I didn't have) to make out for two days straight. I also wanted to give her some of my peppermint gum. I really hoped that she liked peppermint.

Eleven

Marnie

2:25 PM

Eldon gaped at me the whole time I was dancing, looking completely starstruck. Eventually the music stopped and I picked my cloak back up as I came toward him, passing out a few high-fives in the process.

"Wow," he said. "Marnie, you're really good."

"Thanks. I don't often dance in front of people but it's fun. Can't help moving to catchy music."

"I like music," he said. "But I don't dance."

"Yeah." I saw the concern on his face and wondered what he was thinking. "You good?"

"Sorry, Marnie. I don't mean to ogle you, but…sorry. I'm not used to talking this much to anyone. I feel like I keep rambling. But you're easy to talk to." Eldon was trembling as he ran his hands through his hair and his face turned red.

His cuteness is melting me.

"Sorry," he said. "I just don't like stumbling over my words."

"It's okay."

"Your dancing is incredible. I can't believe how you can move."

"Thank you. I can do other stuff too though."

"I figure that," he said.

"So, I was gonna get some coffee and write my book for a bit. You feel like getting coffee too? Maybe write more chapters about your epic Jaeger Bowen?"

"Off campus?"

I smiled when he tilted his head at me. "Yeah," I said. "That spot on Seamoar Drive."

"Sure." Eldon looked from my eyes to my chest. Then he quickly looked down at my shoes. "I'd love a coffee with you, Marnie."

Twelve

Eldon

2:59 PM. Blue Java Beatz Coffee

A shadow of dread hit me once we went inside the coffee shop. *Who is gonna pay? Do I pay for her? Does she pay for us because she asked me out for coffee? No. No, she would pay for herself. We are just friends. Hardly friends. This is not a date. But...I am an elvish gentleman.*

"Uh, Marnie?"

"Yeah?"

"Do you want me to..." I found myself torn between being a gentleman or being Mr. Smooth And Cool when ordering. If I took this long to ask if I should pay for her coffee, then I would forget what I was going to order for myself.

"What?" she asked while looking back at me.

The line is moving. Shoot. I hate ordering things in person. Can never get it out without stammering.

Marnie went from looking sweetly at me to wildly clawing through her purse. I loved how she had her everyday purse on one shoulder and her bulky laptop bag slung over the other.

"Never mind," I said.

She half-smiled at me and ordered herself a strong, black coffee, then walked toward an open table. But she didn't sit down. *Aww. She's waiting for me to get my drink before sitting down. So sweet.* But I quickly scolded my brain. I hated feeling so gushy. *It's not cool, Eldon. Dude. You are such a sap.*

I waited for my iced white mocha, rocking back and forth as I always did when forcing myself to contain my anxiety. *Okay, why do I feel so awkward right now? I should've paid for hers. But I really like her and I'm leaving California after graduation. I don't want to be so attached.*

Thirteen

Marnie

3:19 PM

I guess I could've had him pay or I pay for the both of us. But we aren't a couple. He isn't my boyfriend. Not yet anyway.

Eldon took off his long, theatrical coat and placed it over the chair before sitting down. He was wearing a plain black t-shirt and a subtle cross necklace on a leather cord. *Attractive.* On the casual end of the spectrum as far as fashion went, but very hot. He just stunned me moment by moment.

If a white horse had galloped in and Eldon suddenly told me he had to go fight in a war against goblins and giant trolls, I more than likely would have believed it. *Not all girls have a thing for guys with long blond hair and blue eyes. And maybe not all are into the social awkwardness or old-fashioned mindset. But I'm high right now. So high on what still feels like a dream that I'm going to wake up from tomorrow morning and wish I was forever lost in his eyes.*

Fourteen

Eldon

3:24 PM

Marnie set up her laptop, tablet, and phone, taking up the whole other side of the table. I couldn't help but smirk. "You like machines, don't you?"

"It's faster," she said.

I proudly held up my pencil, feeling a wave of playfulness course through me as I said to her, "This, Arrowswan, is more efficient. And cheaper."

"For you, Jaeger, sure," she said from behind her laptop.

Jaeger, I thought. She called me by my character name. *I love how it sounds coming from her mouth. I'm her Jaeger Bowen. She's my Arrowswan.*

Marnie started typing ferociously, her enthusiasm nearly rattling the laptop off the edge. I grinned. *I love seeing how another writer works.*

She then pulled out a stack of spiral notebooks all squished inside her laptop bag and frantically rifled through the pages.

"What's wrong?"

"The scene I wrote," she said. "The end scene. It was perfect and it's not in here!"

"Then you're allowed to freak out," I said. "From one writer to another, it's totally understood."

"Fudge crackers! Augh!"

I glanced up from my notebook. Marnie had her fingers wound in her hair, pulling on it as if the curly strands would give her extra creative energy. "Can you not work on a different scene?" I asked.

"But I was rearranging the last sentences. It sounded so good!"

I sipped the last of my mocha with my soggy paper straw. *I hate tasting paper.* "I don't write the ending first," I said. "I write the middle."

She looked at me like I just sprouted iridescent wings. "Who starts with middles?"

I raised my hand, staring back with a blank expression, knowing she would find it funny. "Me," I said.

"Writing the middle is the hardest part."

"No," I said. "Not if you know my trick."

Fifteen

Marnie

4:01 PM

"It's like this, Marnie," Eldon said. He used his hands for emphasis as he went into his explanation. "You're on a roller coaster, right? It starts off slow for five seconds and then suddenly you are shot off like a rocket. The best rides include the maximum air time and loops in between the start and stop. Shouldn't the middle of a book be the most exciting part? So exciting that it makes the reader avoid doing anything other than forging ahead to the smashing conclusion?"

Okay. Really. I could listen to this guy talk all day. I stared at his mouth as he talked, noting how shy he was about showing his teeth. *I'm guessing that despite his partial dentures looking and fitting well, he was still not happy about having them. The way he gestures, the way his head tilts to the side and his long hair shines under any bit of light...the way he stumbles over his words as he tries to get it out as fast as he can. I mean, how cute can you get?*

I wanted to respond to Eldon, but I felt an overwhelming urge for something sugary to go with my coffee. And I also needed a second coffee anyway since I was two sips away from finishing my current one.

"Hey," I said, standing up. "I'm gonna get a blueberry muffin. Want me to get you one?"

"Nah," Eldon said. "It's okay."

"All right." I made sure he was sure by giving him a long look before going to the counter. *Maybe he doesn't feel cool, but he is so, so cool. Such an epic vibe.* Walking back to the table, I watched Eldon write something down. He was talking to himself.

"Eldon," I said, setting my muffin on top of my keyboard, "I hate to pour rain on your theory, but I've heard that the least exciting place to sit on a roller coaster is the middle of it."

"I was talking about the track though."

"I still hate writing middles."

He grinned and held his notebook up to his face. "Okay."

I typed a bit more, basking in the coffee shop ambiance and the fact that I had a modern day Elf prince sitting across from me indulging in his own story. "Eldon," I said, "have you published anything yet?"

"Unfortunately no. Too busy trying to make my parents happy."

"Oh… they don't think writing books is a real career?"

"It's more complicated than that." He sighed, tugging on one of his gold hoop earrings. "I really want to write movies, but I don't feel like switching to film school when I'm so close to getting a degree. And…"

"And what?" I asked. I could see that he didn't want to tell me, but I was still curious. Still curious about every aspect of who he was, what he liked, and what he really wanted.

"Long story short, Marnie, I'm screwed if I don't take the job that my mom lined up for me after school. My parents have been paying for my college, but only if I agreed to do things their way."

Oh man, I thought. *That's horrible. And what if I end up marrying this guy? His mom sounds like a hard bit to deal with… and I have a fear of dealing with in-laws. God really needs to give me strength if I have to stand against such a whirlwind of a mother. Yikes.*

But I didn't say anything on the topic because I couldn't relate to that problem. My parents had supported me and my sister every step of the way of our lives and dreams. Whenever I was confronted with a tough or depressing subject, my strategy was to deflect and distract. So I did.

"Tell me more about Jaeger Bowen," I said. "I love that name by the way. Does he look like you?"

"Yeah," Eldon said. He had a faraway look in his eyes and I could only guess that he was still thinking about the conflict with his parents and future job.

"So, Jaeger has long blond hair and blue eyes?"

"Jaeger Bowen," Eldon corrected. " And yes, he does." He looked at me, half-smiling over his notebook. But it was a forced smile. "Does Arrowswan look like you?" he asked.

"She does." I took a bite of my muffin, sending crumbs into the corners of my keyboard. "Where does your character live?"

At that question, Eldon sat up straighter and flipped to a new page, turning it to show me the words written in all caps in bright red ink. "His official title is Jaeger Bowen, Elf Hero of The Aetlanir Sea."

My heart lifted at his point blank enthusiasm for his story character. I couldn't believe I had met a guy who wrote the same kind of things that I did. "Arrowswan hails from the magical country Ranefire," I said proudly. "She is the princess of Ranefire."

"Pretty names," he said. "Do you often buy new books?"

"I like to buy used books. They aren't even that used half the time." I smiled. "I just call them well-loved."

"So..." Eldon said, trailing off. He laid his notebook down and drummed his fingers on the side of the table. He looked into my eyes and quickly looked away, talking toward the empty table next to us. "You ever go to the bookstore a few blocks down?"

"Sure. I love that place. Wanna meet there tomorrow morning? Ten-thirty? I don't have class again until Wednesday."

"I don't either," he said, getting even more fidgety. He ran his hands through his hair in the most awkward but sexy way.

Eldon....my goodness, I thought. *I'm fangirling over you.*

"Not a date," I said firmly as we stood up. I don't know why I had to say that, but it felt like I needed to in order to keep us in the platonic realm. If I gave into the feelings that I had at that moment, I knew there would be a hot, tingly, wild-eyed mess to clean up. And I didn't want to be the girl who pushed a guy into the fast lane. *No rush. This isn't a race, Marnie.*

"Not a date," Eldon agreed in a soft voice.

It can't be a date. It can't. We're just hanging out. I'll be jinxing myself if I call it anything else.

Sixteen

Eldon

5:03 PM. Morro Bay, CA

I figured that since Mark and Geoff wanted to try and make me go out drinking with them, I'd find them alert and ready to kidnap me when I came through the door. But luckily I saw that Geoff wasn't on the couch, and Mark was sitting there instead, taking up the entire coffee table with a miniature battlefield replica.

"Hey, man."

"Hey," Mark said, keeping his eyes fixed on his project.

"Where's Geoff?"

"Out with girls like usual."

"And?" I went to get a bottle of water from the fridge.

"And what?"

"You didn't go with him?"

"If you don't have to go, I sure don't, El."

Fair point, I thought. I looked around at our shared apartment, surprised that it didn't smell like a dead rat. Being a two bedroom, one bath, it was barely enough space for us three guys on a daily basis as we all had our own unpleasant habits. And I had taken the smaller of the two bedrooms… which felt more like a closet at times. Mark had the bigger room and Geoff just slept on the couch.

"Okay," I said. "I'm gonna power down then." *And for real… despite it only being five o'clock, I'm feeling so worn out.*

"El, wait."

I turned, opening my bedroom door. "What?"

"What's that look in your eyes?" Mark asked.

"What look?"

"Man, don't even lie. We've been bros since second grade. You have that goofy, spacing-out look."

"A girl," I muttered, closing and locking the door before he could ask anything else.

"Oh!" Mark's voice jumped a big octave as he tried to get me to talk more. "What does she look like? Does she have blue eyes? Brown? Curly hair? What's her name?"

I groaned, falling onto the bed that my six foot three stature didn't quite fit on. *Go away, dude,* I thought. *She might not even be a real thing. She might just be a dream.*

Mark and Geoff had been my best friends since elementary school, both of them standing up for me during the many years of bullying that I endured, but they also pressured me to get a girlfriend and do any and all trendy sorts of things whether it be good or bad. Sometimes they also were bullies themselves, picking on me for the high standards that I held onto with an iron grip. But I wanted to find my future love on my own and without their help. I didn't want to settle for anything less.

"Marnie," I whispered to myself, smiling at the sound of her name. I stared up at the ceiling, Coldplay blasting through my headphones. *I just want to hug her,* I thought. *Just one hug.*

Seventeen

Marnie

5:17 PM

"Hey, Marnie," Bristol said as I walked into our apartment.

"Hey."

I saw that she was busy playing one of her favorite racing games on the Xbox, and thought about not mentioning Eldon. *But I have to tell her. She's my sister. She will appreciate it.* "Fun fact," I said, dropping next to her on the couch. "I talked to a cute guy and he talked back to me."

"Did he look like Legolas?" she asked, her eyes still on the screen.

"How did you know that?"

She grinned, paused the game, and looked at me. "It's always a guy with long hair. That's your type."

"Maybe," I said. "It's your type too though. Doesn't Terence have long hair?"

Nineteen-year-old Bristol looked coy as she took out her phone and scrolled through pictures of her and her boyfriend. "He trimmed it. It's shoulder-length now."

"Still looks like a warrior, huh?" I said.

"Yeah."

"Of course." I rolled my eyes as I got up to investigate the cupboards. "Did you have dinner yet?"

"No. Feel like making something? I'm just chilling before I work on another painting for a client."

"Client," I said. "Sounds kinda sleazy when you say that."

"They are though. Anyone who commissions me is called a client."

Hearing Bristol get annoyed about my being protective of her, I decided not to push it again.

"I hope this guy isn't another jerk in disguise," I said of Eldon.

"Yeah." Bristol came behind me, taking out a bag of tortilla chips. She caught a runaway jar of peanut butter as it slid toward my face. "You've had bad luck, Marn."

"We should just eat chips and dip," I said.

Bristol shrugged as she brought the chips back to the couch, and I went into the fridge to pull out two containers of bean dip.

"So, do I get to hear his name?" she asked me.

"Eldon," I said.

She smiled. "That's totally an elvish-sounding name. You hanging out again tomorrow?"

"Obviously we are. He loves writing and books too."

"Let me guess. You're going to the bookstore?"

"We are, Bristol," I said. "It's gonna be the best book-hunting day ever."

She handed the chips to me and jumped back into her gaming. "Well," she said, "I hope your Eldon is actually a good guy this time."

I felt dizzy at hearing someone else say his name. *MY Eldon. What if he really was meant to be mine? I'd be the luckiest girl in the universe.*

Eighteen

Eldon

Tuesday, September 18th, 2012. 9:50 AM

"El, where you going? You don't have class today."

I glanced at Mark who was on his second bowl of chocolate cereal. The fact that he thought it was his business to ask about my comings and goings was irritating, but he didn't have much else to think about beyond his miniature model kits and studying to be a math professor. I guess I should've been more flattered that he found me so interesting.

"I'm going to the bookstore."

"Yeah? With the girl you just met?"

"You don't need to know, man."

"Yes, we do." Geoff popped up from the couch, a blue fleece blanket draped over his head. He was in his "unfortunate" typical morning state of messy hair and no clothes. I always preferred that he wore a shirt and boxers when hanging around the apartment, but the guy was not timid or moral.

"No, Geoff," I said. "The last thing you need to know is who I'm hanging out with or her name."

"Okay, I'm gonna guess then."

"I'd rather you didn't." Even though I planned on having coffee at the bookstore, I automatically poured myself a mug as I talked with Geoff. I drank it as fast as I could without severely burning my mouth, standing with my back to the fridge.

"Sheila," Geoff said.

"Nope."

"Whitney."

"Nope again."

"Melissa."

"No," I said. I dumped the rest of my coffee out and headed for the door. "See you guys."

"Wait!" Geoff shouted. "El, wait!"

I looked back to see him grinning with his arms in the air, blanket still on his head. *C'mon, dude,* I thought. *Put on some clothes.* "What, Geoff?"

"Misty!" he said.

I frowned, shook my head, and went out the door. *If I want to bring Marnie around here, I'm gonna have to make sure Geoff's at least half-covered. All the best, most royal environment for the most beautiful girl in the world.*

Nineteen

Marnie

10:35 AM. Bayside's Tomes And Opus Bookstore

I went in ahead of Eldon, beyond excited that he loved books too. *Always extra magical to be in a bookstore that's set just thirty steps from the ocean. Coming in from the cold, salty air and breathing in the yellowed but beloved pages of perhaps a thousand or two thousand books. Heaven on Earth.* The thought of us perusing different genres and then meeting in the middle for one of Jen's over-the-top mochas…that put me into a hyper, almost loopy state of mind. And then I wondered, *How come we never saw each other in the store before?*

"Hi, Marnie, how's it going?" Jen called out from behind her computer screen.

"Good," I said. "Just came in for my weekly therapy."

"Therapy?" Eldon said with a little laugh.

"Yeah. Isn't being surrounded by books and smelling their pages therapy for you too?"

He stood next to me, glancing up at the rows of bookshelves. "Yeah, Marnie, but I don't think I've heard someone actually voice it that way.

You're an otter of a different fur."

I coughed to hide my giggle. *Otter of a different fur. Guess I just learned another of Eldon's backward idioms.*

"How's it going, Eldon? Looking for anything specific today?"

Jen walked past us with an armload of books and set them down on a table near the back of the store. She looked curiously at me and back at Eldon. "You two have come into my store so many times separately and now you're actually in here together. How'd that happen?"

"Well…" I looked toward Eldon who had a no-nonsense, prepare-for-battle face. "Yeah," I said. "We met on campus. Lived in the same area for years but somehow we didn't cross paths until now."

"That's crazy," Jen said. "And you're both about to graduate, right? Next spring?"

"Yup," Eldon said. He smiled at her.

Ugh. That timid, close-mouthed smile, El. You're killing me. How can one guy in my immediate vicinity be so darn adorable and sexy and drive me absolutely insane? My heart feels like it's being lifted up through the eye of a tornado and it's just waiting to be dropped hard into the ground.

Eldon moved on toward the military history section, surprising me with a wink when I went past him.

Ohhhhh, stylin', gorgeous Elf prince... Do you know what you're doing to me right now?

"So, I know that you're close to finishing your next book, Marnie," Jen was saying.

"Yeah," I said.

"Still going the indie publishing route?"

"I am. I love having control of the process."

"Definitely bring in some copies of it when you're done. I'll let you do a book signing here."

I almost smiled, but nerves took over my stomach. Being in my favorite place ever plus having the hottest guy there with me and also talking about my future plans as an author…all of it formed a happy-overwhelmed rush. *A flock of giant butterflies bounce in my chest as I think about what's yet to come. And I hope Eldon will be there for that. Book signing. Yep. That's one of my big writer's life goals.*

"Marnie! You didn't tell me you were that close to publishing another one."

Eldon's voice made me jump. He was standing close to me again, the ends of his hair touching my arm as he leaned down to pour himself some of the free black coffee. His hair smelled so, so good. The sexy smell was stronger than it had been yesterday in class, which meant he added a little extra of whatever he put in it. It was like he had some magical Elf shampoo or gel. *I'd love to run my hands through those long blond locks. Cue the goosebumps and the gooey-ooey cheesy, my-prince-will-come-for-me sigh.*

"Oh, Eldon, you don't want that," Jen said. "It's been sitting out." She waved him away from the red and black coffee vestibule, telling him she would make a fresh pot. But Eldon shrugged at her fluttery, mothering behavior and still drank what he had poured.

"You're that far along with *Arrowswan?*" he asked me.

"Yeah. But I'm writing two books at once. The other one is called *Wailden's Tenth Galaxy.*"

"You gonna tell me about that one? Is it sci-fi?"

"Yes," I said. "The title has that vibe, huh?"

"It does," he said. "Sounds really cool. Was that the one you were working on yesterday at our coffee place?"

Swoon. He called Blue Java Beatz OUR coffee place. We only met yesterday morning and this is just the best freaking week ever. Okay. I gotta stop these thoughts. I'm annoying my own brain. How the crap am I gonna get any studying done?

Twenty

Eldon

11:18 AM

"Yeah," Marnie said. "I was working on my new one."

I automatically looked her up and down, mad at myself for appearing shallow, but she looked so cute with her blue tiara nestled in the midst of her red hair...and how her curls fell over her ears with such a soft, royal flair. She wore a long red coat over her fitted shirt and jeans instead of the silver cloak from yesterday, but it had the same elvish vibe. *Regal. Marnie is vivacious, hot, and regal. Gotta find out what kind of gum she likes. Or...maybe I can just play some of that music she danced to. If only I could charm her by dancing like those guys from her running class. Auggh. There's not a chance I could learn rhythm before graduation! Wish I was as smooth as cream cheese frosting.*

"Cool," I said. And then I said something really dumb. "Do you like cream cheese frosting?"

"What?"

Oh shoot. Oh no. Why did I just ask that?

"Do you like it?" I said again.

Boyo, you need to back up. Get cream cheese frosting out of your head.

"Only if the cheese overrides the cream." Marnie looked at a spot in the ceiling before turning and grinning at me. "You wanna get some red velvet cake next door? It's got the best cream cheese frosting."

Not a date. Not a date. But food is closer to a date. Cake vs coffee? Not ready for more than a coffee place. We're just hanging out. Maybe... maybe she could come over to my place? Just hanging out. That's all we're doing.

"Sorry," I said. My thoughts were pinging all over the place. More up in the clouds than usual. "I don't know why I said that. I'm good actually. I think I need to get home and study. Maybe read more of that massive Latin book I promised my dad I'd get through." *Ohhhh. I am such an idiot. Why am I fumbling so much today? I'm not going to ask her out.*

Marnie looked a little deflated but she didn't lose the sparkle in her eyes. "No worries."

"But do you want to hang out on Friday?"

"Okay. Where at?"

"My apartment." *It's not a date. I'm totally not asking her out.*

"Really?" she said.

"Not to do anything. Just chill."

The smirk on her face made me backtrack. *"Chill" doesn't mean what it should mean. Shoot, Eldon.* "Well," I said, trying not to stammer, "can I show you my storyboarding technique on my computer?"

"Yeah." She glanced at her phone as she answered me, but didn't question why I don't just use a laptop. "That sounds cool."

"I have a couple roommates." I pushed the door open for her to walk out first. "But usually they don't get in the way." *Okay. Total lie right there. Oops.*

"It's okay," she said. "I live with my sister. Splitting the rent on an apartment. Kinda irritating to not have my own space either but it is what it is. Can't afford privacy these days."

"Yeah," I agreed. "But I'm typically a homebody. Hopefully you're okay with that."

"Yeah, I can tell that you're not a huge fan of public spaces. Not a bad thing though," she said. "I like my solitude when I can get it."

"I don't mind public spaces as long as it's not super rowdy or crowded. But same," I said. "I like my quiet time."

We traded small smiles and Marnie looked toward the ocean.

"You like living here?" I asked. "Or would you prefer the mountains? I know you said your dream is to have a lake cabin."

"I love the ocean too," Marnie said. "But I'm definitely a forest girl."

Forest girl, I thought. *Beautiful elvish queen dancing in the trees. That is definitely what she is. Not a princess. A queen. Elvish queen and more. I want her to be more.*

"I'd love to have a cabin one day too," I said. "Lots of land and a porch to drink coffee on."

"Yes. And a porch swing. Has to have a porch swing," she said.

While walking toward our cars, I couldn't help but feel excited about Marnie and I already discussing a future together. So many things seemed the same between us. So many things seemed so perfect.

"Where's your car?" she asked.

"Oh." I pointed to the left of an overflowing trash bin. "The old, crummy van right there. Does the job though."

Taking her keys out, Marnie moved toward a bright blue convertible. "Before you ask," she said, "I promise I'm not rich. This is just one of those things I'm gonna spend my whole life paying off. Really wanted it."

I smiled, loving that my dream girl owned her dream car. And she looked incredible sliding into the driver's seat. "Beautiful," I said, hoping she would believe I was talking about her ride. "I'll see you Friday?"

"Text me the address," she said. "Bye, El."

As she drove off, I stood still in the breeze, my mouth forming the words too late for her to hear. "Bye, Arrowswan."

Twenty-One

Marnie

Friday, September 21st, 2012. 5:30 PM.

"Why am I nervous? Ugh!" I growled at my shaky hands as a fought to activate the hairspray bottle. "We're just friends."

"You're nervous because you like him," Bristol called out from the kitchen.

She's not wrong, I thought as I stared at my reflection. I spritzed my hair, deciding to forgo the emerald green tiara. It felt heavier than normal.

"What time did he say to come over?" Bristol asked.

"I'm going over in a few minutes."

"How long you gonna stay?"

I came out of the bathroom with a sigh, silently praying that my stomach would stop lurching like a tiny raft in the open ocean. "I don't know, Sullie," I said, using my sister's favorite nickname for herself.

"Well," she said, "I'll be on campus in the art department."

"What for?"

"To have more space to make a mess with my oil painting."

49

I secretly rolled my eyes. There was never a mess when she painted. There were other reasons for her to spend the afternoon in the main art building. "Is Terence gonna be there?"

"Only in digital form," she said. "It's my favorite place to video chat with him."

"Okay," I said. "I can't say that's weird or crazy because I'm feeling weird and crazy right now about to go over to a random guy's apartment."

Bristol laughed. "So, he sounds like he's your dream future husband and at the same time you're freaking out that he might be a scumbag?"

"Hey. I'm allowed to be nervous. I can't believe I'm getting to be in his apartment this early in our whole getting to know each other phase."

"How far is he?"

"Not far. Ten minute drive." I smiled at her as I gathered my purse, fishing inside the main pocket for my keys. "He's showing me storyboarding stuff on his computer."

"Storyboarding? Are you serious?"

"Yeah, I'm serious. Apparently he doesn't have a laptop either so—"

"Oh. My. Gosh. Marnie!" Bristol shrieked at me.

"What?"

She nearly hopped off the floor as she said with wide eyes, "I bet he's going to reveal all his bad boy secrets right in front of you!"

Oh c'mon, I thought. But in that moment I knew my sister was messing with me, because her startled expression switched into a giddy, mischievous grin, and we both started giggling.

It took me way too long to get out the door that afternoon… but by the time I drove to the address Eldon texted, I knew I had no regrets about coming over. *I'm in for something special,* I told myself as I took several long breaths before stepping out of my car. *Just don't trip, Marnie. Whatever you do, do not let your first time walking up the steps to*

Eldon's apartment be the time where your balance fails you.

Twenty-Two

Eldon

6:02 PM

I was so excited when I successfully welcomed Marnie into the apartment without my friends butting in. We made it to my room, my odd self trying to be cool by pointing out all the mundane features of the space along the way, and I sat down at my computer. Marnie stood behind me, looking over my shoulder to see what I was doing.

"Do you really not have a laptop?" she asked.

"I really don't," I said. "Helps keep my computer time limited when I just have a desktop."

"Smart."

I wasn't sure if she was being sarcastic but I'm glad she agreed, and having Marnie sitting on the edge of my bed right next to me was probably the new best experience ever.

"Hey, Marnie," I said, "do you mind plugging my lava lamp back in?"

I felt like I needed extra inspiration when I showed her all the work I had done on my story, so I pointed to the lava lamp that was turned off. Then I gestured under my desk. "I like the light and motion when

I'm in my writing mode. The outlet's right there."

"Yeah. Hang on."

It occurred to me as Marnie ducked under the desk that I was being a bit ungentlemanly by asking her to do such a thing for me when I was also capable of bending down to plug the lamp in… but something about watching her get down like she did and have a moment on her hands and knees… it got me all goopy.

This girl is so adorable and so elegant in everything she does, I thought. *Her form is just magic.*

But I did make a big mistake when I led Marnie into my room. I forgot to close the door. Marnie was just about to crawl back out from under the desk, her face next to my legs, when I heard Geoff's voice boom out: "Wow, El! You could've told me you two were in the middle of swapping—"

"NO!" The horror and embarrassment of what Geoff was thinking sent me into a frenzy. I struggled to get out of the chair as I tipped backward, falling with it onto the floor.

Marnie's explosive giggle outburst calmed my panic for a second, but then I thought about how Geoff was still standing in my doorway in nothing but boxers.

"Geoff!" I yelled indignantly as I got up.

Both Geoff and Marnie were laughing hard at my clumsy episode.

"Could you please put some clothes on?" I asked Geoff. "Seriously, man."

"For the girl, sure," Geoff said in a very dismissive, I-didn't-really-hear-you voice. He went to the kitchen and Marnie followed him. "Fun way to meet someone," she was saying.

I smoothed my hair as I joined them, still wanting to show Marnie my storyboard stuff on my computer, but seeing that she was entertained by Geoff, I figured I had to switch gears. "Do you feel like watching a movie?" I asked her.

"Yeah, that sounds good."

"So, you're the girl he met in his art class," Geoff said with a big grin, offering her a package of string cheese. "I'm Geoff."

"Marnie," she said, accepting the cheese while keeping her eyes above the obvious danger zone.

"Marnie. I like that. Well, I hope you don't mind if I have a chat with the girlfriend. I'll be outside on the stairs."

I sighed, relieved that he wasn't going to continue walking around in his boxers in front of Marnie. But the fact that he was unashamed to do that outside of our apartment… wacky.

"What movie you feel like?" I asked Marnie. "And before you pass judgment, yes, I do use DVDs."

"Really?" Her eyes grew big as she saw the giant binder I picked up out of the living room shelves. "Do you collect them?"

"Yeah." I smiled at her excitement. "You like the old school way of watching movies too?"

"Yeah. Ooh! *A Bug's Life*! That's my favorite kids movie of all time!"

My jaw dropped. *Same taste in movies?* "No way. That's my favorite too! I've seen it probably five hundred times since childhood."

"Well…" Marnie sat back on the couch. "Besides the obvious king of favorite movies, *The Lord Of The Rings*. THAT trilogy is my life."

"Same," I said. After popping *A Bug's Life* into the player, I went to sit near Marnie, but was overcome with anxiety about awkwardly or accidentally touching her. I sat on the floor instead, hearing her soft breathing behind me. *This isn't a date*, I told myself as the colorful, silly-adventurous movie started. *We're just hanging out. But man. Hanging out with a beautiful girl doesn't feel casual. It feels like an honor. An honor I couldn't have prayed any harder for.*

"Girl, you gotta be kidding me!" Geoff came back into the apartment, holding his phone up to his face. Still video chatting. "No. No, you ain't playing! Dang, Shanre. You're freakin' hot in that!"

Okay, okay. Eldon, do not blow up at Geoff. You'll just make it worse. Just ignore him. Marnie's ignoring him. Or she seems to be.

Geoff paced around, talking and laughing loudly with his girlfriend who I knew was only one of many in his world. It was a normal day for me, but I wondered how Marnie was processing the sight of it.

Twenty-Three

Marnie

6:30 PM

As much as I wanted to be totally alone with Eldon, I didn't want to appear desperate or obsessed. And I loved hanging out with guys in general. Guy humor and bathroom humor was up my alley. *And Eldon has yet to know that about me.*

Watching Eldon on the floor, I found myself intensely attracted to the length and shape of his legs. And the way he propped himself up against the couch. Even the look of his neutral black socks and the way his feet were positioned made me tingly. He was so like a model in that moment.

I don't know why but I really wish he would turn around and cup my chin in his hands and just kiss me hard. I know I'm romanticizing him. I know I should wait for the flaws to appear. But all I'm seeing right now is a guy that I want to be trapped in a hotel room with.

At one point Eldon got up, went to the kitchen, and came back with a plastic jar of peanut butter and a spoon. He started eating it, taking very small bites, right out of the jar. That drove me nuts in the best way.

"Want some?" Eldon asked with a glance over his shoulder.

"No, thanks," I said.

I did enjoy watching the movie with Eldon, but it was distracting to see Geoff walk around in his boxers while video chatting with some girl.

"Hey, man," Eldon said to Geoff. "What happened to putting on clothes?"

"I'll put on a shirt after I'm done talking with Shanre. And anyways, the boxers cover what needs to be covered." He gestured to me. "Marnie's not cussing me out so she must be chill with it."

No, dude, I thought. *I do actually feel awkward.*

"Could you at least face the other way?" Eldon asked Geoff, making a twirly motion in the air with his spoon.

Geoff shook his head, silently pointing to his phone that he held right up to his eyes. Then Eldon made a hilarious, disgusted face at Geoff that would have had me rofl'ng if I hadn't been trying to act so chill. He groaned and went back to scooping his peanut butter, scraping the excess back into the jar whenever he took a bite.

"You sure you don't want any peanut butter, Marnie? I have another jar of it."

"No, I'm good."

But the crazy part of me wanted to eat peanut butter right off Eldon's spoon while staring into his eyes. I'd drown in the blue magic of his irises and beg for more. *More peanut butter. Some hands-on affection. Maybe a little slow dancing in the dark.*

"You okay, Marn? Story idea?"

"What?"

Eldon was looking back at me. "You're staring at the ceiling. Seen this movie one too many times, huh?"

"No, I do love it. It's good. I'm good."

"I'm messing with you," he said in his dry humor way. He put the spoon in the jar, placing it on the table, and got off the floor. He pointed to the couch. "Mind if I sit next to you? I don't want to crowd your space."

"Yeah." I smiled at him as he sat to the left of me. I was SO happy.

Twenty-Four

Eldon

7:20 PM

I'm sitting next to my biggest crush I've ever had on the couch. The couch that is stained with way too many offensive things. The springs are squeaking a lot. Shoot. We really need to upgrade.

I felt like a character in *The Sims* game. Like I just had a bubble pop above my head with an angry emotion in it because the comfort or aesthetic level of the couch didn't satisfy me. *Too bad I can't read Marnie's mind to see if she is feeling comfortable or not. If I was really Jaeger Bowen, I would have the power to read her thoughts. Darn.*

"All right, you two. Movie's almost over." Geoff collapsed into the couch, falling against Marnie. "I get to pick the next one. Something with car chases and explosions."

"Since when do you watch movies?" I asked. "And why did the video chat end?"

"Oh. She had to help her friend's cousin move some furniture or something. I don't know. But dang, she's a strong girl. Strongest girl I've been out with."

I saw Marnie trying to hide a smile, realizing she was amused at Geoff's rambling.

"How about you go back outside, Geoff, and Marnie and I pick our next movie?"

Geoff looked like he was ready to bark out a raucous response, but the rattling noise of keys outside the front door stopped him. *Oh great, I thought. Mark's back now too.*

Mark came in with an armload of grocery bags. Every single one of those bags, I knew, was full of the junk food that my body couldn't handle without excess gas and stomach cramping. He looked straight at Marnie and shouted in a crazy, high-pitched voice, "That's the girl?!"

"She is," I said. "Mark, this is—"

"No, I know who she is! Marnie! She's the girl who did that epic shuffle dance video!"

What? I thought. Marnie's that famous online? Oh no... all these dudes must be going wild for her and how she can move all sexy.

"Is she really?" Geoff looked at Marnie with excited eyes. "That's so awesome."

"I dance a little bit," Marnie said. "But it's not like my job or something."

"Girl," Mark said, "you're a rock star!"

I could tell she was glowing from all the attention, but it worried me. *They are good looking guys too.* Geoff still showing off his gym rat physique and Mark with his cool tan complexion and wavy hair. I wanted to kick Mark when he forcefully sat himself between Marnie and Geoff. He nearly made me fall off the other end of the couch.

"Marnie, seriously. I love that you can dance. My brother makes music videos like with all the hot models and stuff and the music is always insane club beats."

I didn't know what to think when Mark got on a tangent like that. It was weird how he could go from studious geek poring over math books to acting like a fanboy over a crazy pretty girl.

"Hey, Marnie," Mark said, "do you like wine? We should all go to Sybil's Anchor. It's Friday night, so we shouldn't just sit around here. And we can finally get Eldon to go out because he almost never comes with us anymore to the bars."

"You know I don't like drinking, Mark," I said firmly.

"I don't have any other plans," Marnie said, looking at all three of us guys. "I'd love a drink."

I face-palmed myself inside my head when she said that. *Now I have to be the designated driver. And there's no way in the world I'm letting her go out alone with those two.*

"Okay, El." Geoff hopped up, aiming for the door. "We'll be waiting in your van."

"Thanks," I said sarcastically. I blew out a sigh, looking sideways at Marnie. "Sure you wanna go?"

"Yeah. Long as I get plenty of food in me I can hold down my alcohol," she said with a wink and sly smile.

Oh my, I thought. My hand immediately pressed to my chest as I felt the surge of butterflies. *I'm in trouble if this girl gets drunk.*

* * *

The drive to Sybil's Anchor was short and unbearably loud. Geoff had insisted that we listen to rap music in my van, and though I generally kept to a rule that said the driver is the one who picks the music, I let him have his moment of glory. Mostly because I didn't want Marnie to think I was a total killjoy. *On edge. That's how I'm feeling now.* Especially when we were going to a restaurant that was notorious for its variety of alcoholic beverages.

"You keep a really neat car," Marnie had said when she got into the front passenger seat. She laughed when the rap music exploded through the crappy speakers, and I cringed at Geoff's howling along with the lyrics that definitely did not need to be echoed.

For all the dorky and light-hearted mannerisms that Marnie has shown me, she sure is the most easy-going girl I've known in the face of immoral settings. So modest, yet so nonjudgmental. The way she is embracing my roommates is cute... however, I can see she has a wild side. A dangerous line that I'm nervous to cross. My thoughts consumed me as I drove, but I made it to the restaurant, letting Geoff lead us to the bar area where Mark then chose a table for us. Marnie had barely sat down before she ordered herself a big glass of Pinot Noir.

"Oh, and, just for the record," Marnie announced, rising to her feet with glass in hand, "None of you are paying for me. I'm my own wingwoman and my own drink woman."

Twenty-Five

Marnie

8:41 PM

I had not had so much chaotic fun with a group of guys since my high school days. It was such an exciting feeling to be surrounded by laid-back, cute men who all had their own unique vibes. Initially, I found myself talking a mile a minute, which I often did when I was hyper in the middle of a new adventure. But halfway through my first glass of wine, I slowed down, thinking about how uncomfortable Eldon appeared sitting across from me. *I'm not really a wild person*, I wanted to tell him. I just had spurts of feisty in me that spilled over once in awhile.

"You okay?" I asked over the boom of the restaurant's music.

He nodded, going back to dancing his fork around his plate. I know Eldon had mentioned that he was a picky eater, and seeing the particular way he was zig-zagging his fork through the clumps of shrimp and strands of pasta, I thought he might be forcing himself to eat what he usually didn't.

"Marnie!" Geoff bumped me with his elbow as he slid back into his chair. He had been gabbing with the bartender like they were old buddies. "I heard from Mark that Eldon's really into you. More than he's been with any other girl." He put his arm on the back of my chair and leaned in, sipping his beer inches from my face. "And the guy's crushed on a lot."

I subtly moved my chair a few inches away from him, looking at Eldon again. Eldon gave a small smile when I said to Geoff, "I like him too."

* * *

We mostly ate and drank through the next couple of hours, various topics coming up by way of Mark and Geoff and their motormouths. I could see how Eldon would get annoyed by them and how condescending, crass, and brutal they could sound during conversations among themselves. I didn't think too much of their cussing and trash-talking of girls until they turned on me.

"You're really quiet, Marnie. What happened to the crazy dancer freak from the video?"

I had yet to make my way through my third glass of wine, but the unexpected words coming from Mark put me into get-tipsy-to-not-be-angry mode.

"I just don't need to say stuff all the time. If it's stupid and shallow I don't want to share it."

"But stupid and shallow is the best part!" Mark said. He laughed into his margarita, then spit it all over the table. Geoff fell onto him in his own fit of drunken laughter.

"So, you know, Eldon is way more shy than you. I didn't think a girl who dances like that could be so quiet. Why do you both wear pointy ears? You know Elves aren't real, right? Like you don't love to be sexy in your own human body. But you're so spicy hot, Marnie. You should show it off."

Mark was talking to me with saliva dripping from his mouth. His logic was completely gone, poking fun at my personality, yet also saying inappropriate things about my body and how I could use it. *Not fun anymore. I feel like I can't be the cool girl they want me to be... but I don't want to be an idiot. I don't want to get all crazy for them.*

"You're like serious now. You should drink more. You need to drink. Be that fun dancing girl, Marnie. Oooh! I can tell the bar dude to turn the music to a—"

"Mark, no," Eldon said sternly. The deep tone in his voice startled me. It startled all of us.

Twenty-Six

Eldon

11:30 PM

It was terrifying to drive three drunk people back home. Once I made sure that Geoff and Mark got up into our apartment without a painful face plant, I turned to Marnie, realizing she needed me to drive her back to her place. I wasn't going to let her be behind the wheel for even one mile.

"I'm not drunk," she said to me. "I'm fine."

"It's late. I want you to be safe." I could feel my protective nature coming out and felt bad knowing that I might sound like a strict rule-maker.

"It's not that far. I'll be okay."

"Marnie, you had drinks."

"Three glasses," she said with a grin.

"Three and a half." I lightly held onto her arm, keeping her from moving toward her car. "May I please drive you home?"

"But what do I do about my convertible?"

"It'll be safe here. I'll pick you up in the morning," I said. "Then I'll bring you back here to get it. Please? I lost a good friend to a drunk driver and… I just want to make sure you're okay."

I sucked in a breath when Marnie tilted her head at me. She smiled and nodded, agreeing to let me drive.

* * *

"The real world isn't kind to gentle spirits," I said as we pulled out onto the street. "That's what Jaeger Bowen would say."

Marnie turned from the window, giving a totally tipsy smile at me. "Is he always that poetic?"

"Pretty much," I said.

"Do you think I'm crazy?"

"No."

"Do you not wanna hang out anymore?"

Aw, Marnie, I thought. *She thinks that I think she is too wild. That I'm out of her league. Funny thing is that I think that I'm out of HER league… but I would never say it out loud.* "Of course I wanna hang out," I said. "What makes you think I don't?"

She played with her hair as she talked, trying to steady her voice. "You were probably hoping for a more mellow girl. One who doesn't drink. But usually it's the guy who thinks it's fun when the girl gets tipsy."

"I'm not that guy," I said. "I'm the other guy."

"Oh."

"But I don't care if you drink wine once in awhile." I wished so badly I could hold her hand. That I could tell her how wild she drove my mind. "I was just concerned about you and facing off against my friends. I'm sorry they got all idiotic."

"Don't worry," Marnie said. She sighed loudly and looked out the window again. "I know that it was just the alcohol turning them into jerks."

"No. It was more than that. But drinking sure doesn't help."

"Guys always made fun of me in high school. I don't know... I guess I had this false hope that somehow that phase had ended."

Darn. Now I feel really bad for her. And I realized something. Marnie drank more to feel better about herself. I knew so because I had once been on that side. I had given in to the world's pressures. *AKA fitting in.*

"Well, I've never felt as cool as the outgoing, fashionista types," Marnie said. "I don't like doing my nails or getting my hair done. I'm sort of disheveled."

"Marnie, if you're disheveled, then you are a very attractive disheveled."

"Thanks." She smiled at me and I smiled back.

"Just the truth," I said.

With a few short directions from Marnie, I made the journey to her apartment complex, parking a few spaces down from where she had to walk. The sea fog was thick and cold outside, but I loved the cozy vibe it gave as we sat in my van. Romantic. Even though it wasn't a date.

Marnie unbuckled herself and picked her purse up off the floor. "You said you lost a friend to drinking?"

"Yeah." I slowly unwrapped a piece of gum to distract myself from the somber memory. "Him and his mom. They were driving back from a birthday party in Santa Barbara. He was only seventeen."

"I'm sorry. I haven't lost any friends that way."

"He was friends with Mark and Geoff too back in the day. We called ourselves 'masters of the recess war.'"

Marnie laughed, sliding down in the seat. She turned her face to me, brown eyes sparkling. "How old were you guys when you made that up?"

"Elementary age. Young."

"That's so cute," she said.

"So, what do you think?" I asked. "Wanna get out? You should probably get some sleep."

She nodded and opened the car door, taking a few steps toward the stairs. I followed, not wanting to be an annoyance, but wanting to keep her safe. "Your apartment is on the second floor?"

"Yeah. My sister's probably asleep. I got my keys though." Digging through her purse, she said, "You didn't have to take me home, El."

"I wanted to."

"I'm fine though. I ate a lot. Most of it soaked up the wine I think."

"Yes, you did eat a lot," I said with a chuckle. "Very impressive."

Marnie smiled at me. Her keys were in her hand, but she leaned against the door instead of going in. "You're really tall."

"Am I?"

"Standing this close to you, yeah," she said. "Perfect Elf height."

"Thanks." I breathed gently as I watched her study my face. The way her eyes were tracing every part of me like a laser. "And," I said, "you're a perfect Elf queen height."

"Princess," she defiantly said. "Arrowswan's a princess."

"No. Queen. You're a queen."

The wind blew through Marnie's curls and they swept across her face. I instinctively reached out, tucking strands of her hair behind her ear. I felt so bold. So smitten. *Touching her ears, her face. My fingers gliding along her cheek. We barely know each other but it feels like we've always been here. What's gotten into me? I've never been this forward with anyone.*

"Then you should be an Elf king instead of a prince. So we match."

"Reasonable," I said. "Jaeger Bowen will now be a superhero Elf king." Putting my hands in my coat pockets, I decided to make another bold move. It was bold for me at least. "Would you maybe feel like going to the beach tomorrow?"

"Yeah. That sounds fun. We could take a walk or get lunch too."

"So, I can take you to the beach and then after that I'll drive you back to my place to pick up your car?"

"As long as we call it the opposite of a date," she said.

"Not a date." I nodded, fighting the urge not to touch her hair and face again. "Okay. Yeah, I don't want to jinx it."

"Me neither."

"Have a good sleep, Marnie." I turned to head back to my van and then stupidly spun around to throw out a time. "Eleven. I'll pick you up at eleven."

"Just friends," Marnie said firmly. She stood in the middle of her doorway, her cuteness even in her tipsy state making my heart pound like a jackhammer.

"Just friends," I echoed.

"Oh and, Eldon?"

"Yeah?"

"Did you really have something to show me on the computer?"

I could hear the teasing tone in her voice and I smiled as I answered. "Believe it or not, I really did."

She backed into the apartment, giggling before she closed the door. "Show me next time, El."

I will, I thought. *But I think my real life is turning out to be more magical than anything I've written.*

Twenty-Seven

Marnie

Saturday, September 22nd, 2012. 11:15 AM

Sitting next to Eldon as he drove us to the beach, I was feeling less embarrassed than I thought I would be after the previous night of drinking. We both had given obvious hints that we liked each other, but refused to say that we were dating or that we were friends with benefits. *Stay platonic. Because... you know. Prior heartaches and fear of rejection. Totally normal. Not really. But we can't get into all the clingy intense physical stuff. There's no turning back once we go there. Then I'll lose him as a friend. But it did feel amazing when his hand touched my face last night. I had goosebumps on and off for an hour before I finally fell asleep.*

We found out through our on-the-road conversation that neither of us were big on traveling. We liked sticking close to what was safe and familiar, and apparently we were both born and raised in Morro Bay. It was nice to connect with a man who didn't need to travel the world in order to feel accomplished.

I considered all of San Luis Obispo County to be my hometown territory, as did Eldon, and it seemed like our favorite places to hang out were in that same general area. Cambria was only a thirty minute drive from Morro Bay, and I agreed that we should make that our beach spot.

"Does your family still live around here?"

"They live in Atascadero," I said.

"What a coincidence," he said. "My parents own a Christmas tree farm there. They live on it and everything."

"I love Christmas trees. How long have they had the farm?"

"They bought it right before I started college. My dad is retired after managing a hotel chain. My mom is semi-retired we like to say. She's one of those fast-talking, intense-eye-contact-giving busybody ladies."

Surprising that a guy like this would have a mom like that, I thought. *But hey, if he turned out this amazing I suppose I should thank his parents instead of be worried about the potential in-laws nightmare.*

"My dad is an optometrist," I said. "And my mom worked at a bank for a long time. They do a lot of traveling now."

Eldon looked at me as I talked, keeping one hand firm on the wheel. He snapped his gum and glanced in the rear view mirror as he merged into the left lane. "World travelers?" he asked. "Or just in the States?"

"They prefer super long trips all over the world. Global adventures."

"Hm. Yeah, I'm certainly not into gallivanting across countries. Makes me feel like a reindeer without antlers."

I giggled and saw him start to smile as he looked back at the road. *Reindeer without antlers*, I thought. *That must be Eldon-speak for 'fish out of water'.* And I was dying with hotness overload when I looked at his outfit that day. He wore a light green t-shirt and blue jeans, black and white sneakers, sunglasses on the top of his head, and he had a replica of the One Ring on a chain around his neck. And, of course, that long blond hair that looked way too perfect, but it was so shiny and straight and smelled sooooo magical. *Wow. He is so literary and cinametically geeky I can't handle it!*

"Eldon," I said, "you remind me of one of my old story characters I created back in junior high."

"Yeah? What was the character?"

"His name was Eldemar. He was part of this group of Elf doctors that were best friends and they existed in the modern world. You just look so much like him right now."

"Eldemar? That doesn't sound like someone who would resemble me."

"No, he does," I insisted. "He has long blond hair and he drives an ambulance." I realized that I was going off into a totally different topic, but Eldon didn't seem to mind at all. He seemed to love playing along with whatever I talked about.

"Should I become a paramedic then?" Eldon said with a laugh.

"Nope. You're good."

"And do all of your male story characters look like Tolkien's Elves?" he asked.

I bit my lip, facing the window. I was in love with the fact that he knew he was torturing me with his teasing. "Most," I said. "Including you, El. But you're real."

He took his sunglasses from the top of his head and put them on as streams of sunlight pierced through the clouds. "I sure am, Arrowswan."

I loved so much how we could ask each other any question or deviate onto any random topic and we both responded with genuine curiosity and joy. I didn't think he was weird and he didn't think I was weird or prying. The sparks of fascination between us were glowing hard and fast like fireworks in the darkest of nights. It was like God made us for each other. *How else could something so miraculous happen in less than a week?*

Twenty-Eight

Eldon

11:44 AM. Cambria, CA

Marnie eagerly bounded out the door the second that I parked, and I couldn't keep up with her as she jogged onto the sand. Wisps of fog remained in the sky, but it was a beautiful beach day.

"You're very energetic," I said.

"Yeah. Coffee."

"Ah, okay." I stepped next to her as she slowed down. "How about some more getting-to-know-you questions?"

"You ask first," she said.

"Okay. When's your birthday?"

"December sixth."

"Mine's December ninth," I said.

"Favorite holiday?" she asked.

"Christmas."

"Mine too. What's your favorite family tradition at Christmas?"

I had to think long on that one, looking out at the waves while Marnie looked at me. "Watching *The Polar Express* on Christmas Eve, seeing

74

Santa ride down the neighborhood streets on top of the fire truck, and walking down Christmas Tree Row to see all the lights."

"You like seeing Santa too? That's so cute!"

I grinned. "It's part of the magic. And when I was younger, my family always went to the Christmas Eve service at our church. I loved holding a candle while singing carols."

"Me too," Marnie said. "So cozy and comforting."

"For sure."

We sat across from each other on a big, flat rock, and Marnie began picking through the sand to find shells.

"How old are you gonna be?" she asked me.

"Twenty-four."

"I'm gonna be twenty-three."

"One year ahead of you," I said with a wink. Knowing that she was twenty-two going on twenty-three gave me a protective warrior jolt. It was a trivial thing… caring about someone's age. But I liked that I was a year older than her.

"Eldon, I have a super random question for you."

"Tell me."

"Do you ever feel like the world is shallow and cold-hearted toward old souls?"

"Oh my, yes," I said. I slid off the rock, lying down in the sand. It wasn't smooth at all… filled with bits of tiny pebbles and shell fragments. But the coarseness was sort of like a massage. *I'm weird*, I told myself. *I know I am. My thoughts are weird.*

"And do you think it sucks to be in a group of people who boss you around and critique everything you say?"

"Let me guess," I said. "You're referring to all those small group projects we have to endure in classes?"

"YES!" Marnie shouted. She jumped into the air and dropped next to me, sitting a couple inches from where I was lying down. "Can you imagine if people weren't so shallow and judgmental all the time?"

"Yeah," I said, putting my sunglasses back on. "That'd sure be something."

"I mean, imagine the quality conversations one could have."

"Yeah. Most people wanna just talk about who's got the cleanest house, prettiest hair, or who has the better potluck dish at a party."

"Exactly. It's so annoying. Whatever happened to deep, intricate communication?"

We were silent for a few minutes, listening to the waves and our own breathing. Marnie's breath was relaxed. Mine was slowly growing more rapid. Being close to Marnie… smelling whatever conditioner she had in her hair. *This girl is out of this world,* I thought. *So sweet and so HOT. I want to call her my baby. I want her to be mine.*

"You know, Marnie," I said, "I've always been more shy when I'm in a group of people or having to give a speech. But I'm not shy when I'm with you."

"I'm glad we can be ourselves," Marnie said. "It's a relief."

I sat up, brushing sand from my hair. "Everyone says I'm too quiet. They think I don't know how to talk or that I hate them. But I don't hate people. I just prefer silence."

"And they think WE are abnormal. As if anyone is truly normal in the world."

"Modern society makes fun of quiet people."

"Truth," she said. "I think we should fight back."

This little curly-haired spitfire. Man. Listen to her. It's like she's about to lead the charge across a bloody battlefield. Her sexy Elf queen body running toward the snarling goblin army. Sigh. "How?" I asked.

"Let's show them how awkward and strange we really can be. Like just completely blow their minds with an eccentric response to their chattering."

Good idea, Elf queen, I thought. I was thrilled to add a couple cents to her motivational speech. "We act so strange and unnatural that they can do nothing but fall silent themselves and walk away!"

"Render the speakers speechless," she said.

"Yes."

"We can get the dreaded "parting the Red Sea" effect and this time we will think nothing of it."

I grinned, watching her stand and pace around as she talked fast. I loved seeing her get excited about something. "You mean when people create a wide perimeter when we walk in a room because we are so notoriously idiosyncratic?"

"Yeah," she said.

Game on, Arrowswan. I don't care how weird this gets. You're amazing to me.

"Do you ever get mad at how people react to your authentic, not-so-streamlined self?" she asked. She began throwing her arms in the air, gesturing as each sentence came out louder and louder. "Either I talk too much or don't talk enough. And then when I do talk, my thoughts and opinions are irrelevant to the group."

I stood up, following her as she went closer to the water. I tossed my sneakers aside and walked in the damp sand with her. "Exactly," I said. "It's the same thing with me."

"Then what should we call this battle technique?"

I felt so much like I had found the best friend I had waited my whole life for. It was us against the world… scheming and working together to be more confident as gentle spirits in a noisy, harsh world. "Operation Quiet," I said. "Wait. No. Vow Of The Silent Kindred."

"That's so good," Marnie whispered. "The harshness of modern society will sting less when we laugh and stand against it."

VOTSK. Our own special code. Our own secret bond. I grinned wide, unafraid to show my teeth or my flash of bravado. *Best day.*

Twenty-Nine

Marnie

12:35 PM

"What are the rules?" I asked. "Or guidelines rather."

"Paper airplanes," Eldon said. He tossed a round black stone into the ocean. "If the room or space is too big to get a message by handing paper, we write it and throw it to each other."

"My aim is terrible though."

"Don't worry, Marnie. I won't care as long as I can pick it up and read it."

I giggled about the randomness of our discussion. It was too fun. "I think we should make guidelines as we go along."

"Well then," Eldon said, "I can tell you right now, I hate texting. Only in an emergency should we ever text instead of call."

"What? You didn't tell me that."

He tucked hair behind an ear and shrugged. "I didn't want to sound like a picky jerk. But I do prefer real talk on the phone. Just feels better to me."

Aw shoot, I thought. "I hate how my voice sounds on the phone."

"But your voice is soothing, Marn."

Marn. The way he calls me Marn. Oh, my heart. "Okay, Eldon. We'll pass notes on paper. Old school paper and pencil."

Eldon picked up an abandoned Frisbee and we began tossing it to each other as we talked. "We don't have to speak to strangers unless it's a last resort," he said. "Family and friends are necessary to talk to. But if the social gathering is too uncomfortable, then we should break out the arts of distraction."

"Arts of distraction?"

"Yeah." He briefly looked away at a family playing with their dog. A small smile came to his lips. "Let's say, Marnie, that you are dealing with a droning talker or being verbally assaulted by a bossy person. You would signal me and then I would step in with a crazy distraction."

I jumped to the left to make a catch. "But I can't see you doing anything crazy to embarrass yourself on purpose, Eldon."

"For you I will. Within reason."

"Agreed. And we should make up a secret handshake for this whole vow thing."

Eldon held onto the Frisbee as he said, "What if instead of a handshake we wore and showed off a special ring or pendant? We could tell people that we got it at a council meeting."

"A council meeting?"

"Well, you know. Like in *The Lord Of The Rings*. But it's a modern version. That'll be our fun way of saying we share a magical bond. We met and sorted out a secret plan at our council meeting."

"Now you sound the same level of goofy and random as I do," I said with a giggle.

"Thank you, Arrowswan." He half-smiled and bowed before tossing the Frisbee back to me.

"On a tangent, Eldon," I said, "how long have you been obsessed with Elves? I'm surprised you even have the guts to wear pointy ears."

"When I was fourteen, my big brother started calling me 'Magic'. It was during the phase where I talked nonstop about fantasy books and lands. I annoyed my family with my superhero-fantasy hybrid story characters. They thought I had major problems socially, but I was just more comfortable in my own little world. No one gets me the way I would like them to."

"Elves are your safe place, huh?" I said. *Just like me...*

"Sort of, yeah."

"How often do you actually wear the ears?"

"Couple times a week usually." He chuckled when I ducked at his extra hard throw. "What about you?"

"Every day," I said. I threw it back equally as hard.

"I love that, Marnie," he said.

As much as I wanted to make up more specifics for our newly invented Vow Of The Silent Kindred, I had other burning questions for Eldon. Like what other hobbies he had beyond loving Elves and if he liked antiques. Most guys I knew didn't like antique stores but a few did… and they were usually into historical tools or old cars.

"What do you think about people who collect things?" I asked.

"Everyone I know collects something," he said. "I used to collect movie posters and magnets."

"And do you collect anything now?"

"Yep. Vintage postcards. I go to antique stores to find them. And I love old typewriters, but I don't have room to keep any so I just look at them and take in their magical presence."

The geekiness is flying off the charts, I thought. "I collect reindeer and anything with a vintage Santa on it," I said.

"Including ugly Christmas sweaters?" Eldon asked.

"Yeah. I have three Santa sweaters. And I have a light-up fireplace one too. It's funny."

"A fireplace sweater?"

"Yeah. It's this bright retro thing and is super itchy and oversized. I've worn it for various family Christmas gatherings."

Eldon dropped the Frisbee and put his hands in his jeans pockets. He moved away from the water, walking backward. "Do I get to see it this year?"

"Yeah," I said. "I plan on wearing it again. And I'll have my antler and bells headband too."

"Sounds cute, Marnie."

Without voicing it, both of us were feeling the chill of the wind and we went up toward the parking lot. "Do you go to antique stores?" I asked.

"Yup."

"Which ones?"

"I have a favorite," he said. "It's a short drive from here."

"Arkway Treasures?" I asked excitedly.

"Yeah. My family's known the owners forever."

"Yes! Elsa and Abner Reisand!" I said. "I know them too."

"Maybe everyone knows them," Eldon said with a chuckle. "They are very friendly people. And they do talk a lot. I don't think they've ever not been nice to anyone who comes into their store."

I watched him lean against his van, imagining that he was a bad boy in disguise. I, of course, didn't want him to be a real bad boy, but the sight of him in his sporty outfit, sunglasses, and the hair that I couldn't stop drooling over… all of it made me think that he should be putting on a leather jacket and jumping on a motorcycle. But there he was with his van. And he still looked delicious.

"Can we go there for a little bit?"

"Yeah?" he said. "You don't mind putting off picking up your convertible?"

"I don't mind," I said. "If we're out this way right now we may as well keep having fun."

"I'm up for it." He winked as he unlocked the doors. "Hop in, Elf queen."

***

We took the long way to the antique store, blasting the radio, keeping it on the retro (70s and 80s) station. At one point it was "My Sharona" by The Knack that was making me dance, and Eldon turned it up, drumming on the steering wheel. And then the song playing right after it was "I Got You" by Split Enz.

"My favorite old school song!" Eldon shouted.

He rarely raised his voice for anything, so it was cute seeing him get hyper about a song on the radio. We sang it together, trying to harmonize, which was a massive fail.

"You like this stuff too?" he asked me.

"Yeah," I said. "My dad always played it in the house."

Sitting at a red light, all of the van's windows rolled down, a guy next to us in his massive silver truck yelled out the window: "Your girlfriend's freaking hot, bro!"

We looked at each other as he sped off and burst into laughter. I don't know why we found that so funny but we did.

Thirty

Eldon

1:50 PM Arkway Treasures

Marnie and I greeted the store's owners Abner and Elsa as soon as we went inside. They were in their seventies and had grey hair, but they had the most cheerful attitudes about life. Elsa was undeniably spunky and her husband Abner was wide-eyed and chatty as long as he had a mug of black coffee in hand. He always carried the same tan and blue mug around.

"Eldon, I got another Smith Corona in," Abner said. He grinned, waving me over to see the typewriter. I followed him around the corner, hearing Marnie talking with Elsa behind me.

"What color is this one?" I asked. "Is it the baby blue?"

Abner didn't tell me. He just continued to move through the maze of boxes and shelves. The store felt endless depending on which direction you went. A little messy, but full of treasures. That's how I felt about antiques. Treasures from another life.

"Wow," I said when I finally saw it. "It is the blue. I love that."

Leaning on a grandfather clock, Abner brought his mug to his mouth, eyes twinkling as he said, "Elsa's talking Marnie's ear off, isn't she? Want some coffee? You drink it all hours too, right?"

"Not as much as you do, Abner." But I took the paper cup that he offered me.

"So, Eldon, tell me how you and Marnie crossed paths. School?"

"Yep."

"How long you been together?"

"We aren't together. Just friends. We met on Monday."

"Oh?" Abner looked sly as he took a long sip and pointed back toward the front of the store where Marnie was. "You look like you're a match made in Heaven. Haven't seen you smile this much in a few years."

"God must have brought her to me then," I said. The slightest bit of emotion caught in my throat and I coughed to feel normal. "I don't know where else I would've found her."

"Just don't rush things if you wanna keep her around."

"I won't. Trying not to."

Abner was my source of fatherly advice more often than my own dad. Mostly because my dad didn't like talking openly with me about serious life stuff. And in my family, I was the most conservative as far as morals and standards went. My parents thought I was too stringent.

But I chose what I believed in and I did my best to hang onto what I thought was right. With friends like Mark and Geoff, that was always a challenge, but I managed. And I was grateful to have a cool old dude like Abner to chat with. He made me feel okay about myself.

"But a week is pretty fast, Eldon. Even though I knew I wanted to marry my Elsa within a month of meeting her..."

I smiled thinking of how much Abner still adored his wife. I loved seeing couples make it through decades of rough waters and stay together until the end. "I'm not there yet," I said. "I know not to cross that line."

"The kissing line?"

"Yeah. That would be presumptuous. And I'd seem like a player."

"But I know you want to kiss her. Your body language tells all, my man."

"Not to sound corny, Abner, but I've been praying since middle school that He would show me who my future wife is. I want the girl that I fall in love with to be the only one. To be my forever."

"Now you're talking like an elvish warrior poet," Abner said with a wink. "Jaeger Bowen always wanted to find his wife too, didn't he?"

It was comforting to know that Abner didn't think my story characters or ideas were weird. It made it easy to chill and talk with him as if we were blood relatives. "Yeah," I said. "And you know what's crazy? Marnie writes fantasy too. She has a character named Arrowswan, and I haven't told her, but I think Arrowswan and Jaeger Bowen would be perfect for each other."

"It is a God thing," Abner said. He headed back toward the front when we heard the phone ring.

"Well, if she is meant to be mine, I hope He shows me soon."

"He will. He'll tell you in the silence. But I wouldn't let up on pursuing either. Keep learning everything you can about her."

I nodded, sipping my coffee while Abner answered the phone which had a very loud-voiced customer on the other end. He made an annoyed face at me and I laughed before looking around at the corner I was in. More old books. And a rack of postcards. I had a thing about old paper. Any old paper. Touching it, feeling the graininess in my fingers was so satisfying.

Thirty-One

Marnie

2:19 PM

Elsa understood real girl talk. Even at her old age, she could throw out relevant tips for thriving in today's world and knew a thing or two about wading through all the mishy-moshy shallowness of humanity. "It'll happen when you least expect it," she said. "Trust me. That's how Abner asked me out. And a few months later he proposed and I was totally caught off guard."

I sighed, folding my arms next to the register. "Well, I don't think I'm quite ready for that kind of change yet."

"Heaven knows how badly you desire a life partner, hon. Especially a good man like Eldon. Which I really can't blame you for."

We looked toward Eldon as he slowly walked over, coffee in his hand. Even if I just stayed friends with him… close friends… I knew I was lucky. It felt ridiculous to want the guy to be my one true love already. It was exhilarating, terrifying, and my stomach kept switching from dropping fast like a roller coaster to aching from the intense longing and wondering.

"Trust it," Elsa whispered to me. "Trust the timing."

I nodded at her and turned around to smile at Eldon who looked thoroughly curious about what we had just been discussing. "Find any Santa Clauses?" he asked.

"No," I giggled. "But I'm sure when it's closer to Christmas I will."

"Come back in next month," Elsa said. "And for sure we will have more Christmas stuff out. For some reason, late October is the magic time to get the Christmas vibe going."

Eldon put a stack of vintage postcards down on the counter and said in the most out of the blue way, "Marnie, what's your middle name?"

"Staysha," I answered, looking at the cards he had picked.

"Wanna know mine?"

"Sure."

"Fergus."

"Fergus?"

"Eldon Fergus Cornade."

I couldn't help but grin at hearing that. "Marnie Staysha Koehn," I said, wanting to mirror his response.

"Your name is magical," Eldon said.

"Well, I think your full name is hot. In fact..." And then I heard myself say a sentence that was beyond cringeworthy. "If I had a son, I'd name him Halfdan Eldon."

Gurl, my brain screamed at me, *what are you?! Twelve?*

But then Eldon's soft yet masculine voice sounded out. "Really now?"

I looked at where he was standing, bracing myself for what he would say next.

"Halfdan Eldon Cornade?" he said boldly, a teasing smile on his face.

OMG, I thought.

He rifled through a box of CDs on the opposite side of the register while I tried not to squeal out loud.

Swoon. That adorable head tilt he's got going on. And omg he knows I'm talking about maybe one day kids with him...EEE!!!

I blushed hard. And I don't think my cheeks turned to their normal color for the rest of the day.

A lot of people would say they are an open book, but they don't often mean it. Eldon was. He was truly the most open book I'd seen with my own eyes. And if there were secrets he was keeping from me, I told myself that I just wasn't ready to hear them.

Eldon and I were in agreement for a long time that that first week of our meeting and back to back adventures was one of the most thrilling weeks of our lives.

However, what came next... the following couple years... it got stranger and much more... well... our unique definition of awesome.

Thirty-Two

Eldon

Thursday, September 27th, 2012. 12:20 PM. San Luis Obispo, CA

My quirky romantic side is kicking in and I don't know how to shut it off. I'm just slowly pursuing her. Eldon style flirting. No serious grand gestures. We gotta take this slow. Getting to know her. Just getting to know her, Eldon. Breathe and think. Don't be stupid.

"Mark, how do I get girls to stop flirting with me?"

Mark smirked and shook his head as he took a drink of soda. The cafeteria was relatively quiet for being noontime. It unnerved my stomach. "Why make them stop?" he asked. "That's a force you can't really control."

"I only want Marnie's attention," I said. "I'm being chivalrous."

"You can't keep the females from approaching, El. Even if you looked ugly you wouldn't look ugly."

"But they don't like me when I start talking."

"Yeah." He closed his laptop and swiveled to give me his full attention. Which was sort of weird. He had dark owl eyes. "So just keep talking weird then."

"But it's not weird enough. I need to get weirder to repel them away. Especially repelling that one sassy girl who always wears bright, fluorescent clothes."

"Oh!" Mark grinned wide, looking sly. "I know her. Why hasn't she tried to grab my attention?"

I rolled my eyes, figuring I should give him a little unsolicited advice. "Try growing your hair out."

"No," he said. "I can't. It grows vertical. And you need to tame the pretty boy aesthetic, man. Cut the hair, get rugged scruff, and wear baggy clothes."

"No way. I like my Elf look. And Marnie loves it too."

"Then I don't have a solution. And your "problem" is really annoying to the rest of us. Why wasn't I born with that hair?"

I grabbed his arm when he tried to touch the top of my head. I knew he was going to try to undo the epic braid that I spent all morning working on. "Stop it, Mark."

"So? Do you shampoo AND condition?"

"Stop."

"Wow. You really are an Elf prince, Eldon."

"Elf king, Mark. Not prince."

"Sure." He balled up his paper plate as tightly as he could and threw it in the nearest trash can. "Be all the royalty you want."

Seeing how irritated he really was, I wanted to get him to chill out. "Mark, okay."

"Okay what?"

"Wanna go wait with me for Marnie to come out of her class? She has one class on Thursdays and my newest mission is to always be waiting for her outside the classroom door."

"Why would I get excited about that?"

"Because," I said with a sigh, knowing I was venturing into a dangerous situation, "I think I could get her to help you meet a girl who would actually want to hang out with you. A nice one."

Mark didn't look up from his math book, but I saw his mouth twitch and knew that he had heard me.

"Okay, fine!" He slammed it closed and held it under his arm as he stood. "Let's go, Elf king."

* * *

A few steps inside the hall, I saw a pack of flirty hot-as-sunshine girls coming our way, and knew I had to come up with a new method of evading them. I didn't feel like walking or running away that day. I wanted to do something out of my norm. So I looked at Mark who was still engrossed in his math book. "Hey, Mark?"

"What?"

"How comfortable are you with spontaneity?"

He didn't move from his spot against the wall. Nose firmly fixed in the book. A math book of all things. Not an epic tome of space adventures or fantasy worlds. Math. *And to think,* I thought, *that I'm trying to help him get a cute, fun girl. What happened to the guy who was drunk and cracking stupid jokes in the restaurant?*

"What kind of spontaneity, El?" he asked me.

"The humiliating yourself in front of hot girls kind," I said.

"Not very," he said.

The girls were getting closer. I resorted to a move that Jaeger Bowen would use in his story world. "Mark," I whispered, "I just felt an earthquake."

"What?"

"Get down! Earthquake!"

He dropped with me and we both started army crawling as the girls stared. We kept our eyes down as we moved past them. My pulse was racing and my hands were shaking from doing something so dumb and ridiculous.

"There's no earthquake, El. I just followed your lead."

"Thanks, Mark. Way to make me feel better."

"But you never do stupid things like this."

We casually talked while continuing to crawl down the hall, and it didn't hit me until later that we must have looked like quite the goofballs and that we would probably end up online in some viral video.

"Gain a new respect for me?" I asked.

"No, I think you're insane."

"Stay down, Mark. There's more coming."

"More what?"

"Flirty maneaters."

"Oh no," he groaned. "You're not just doing this for Marnie's sake are you?"

"Yeah," I said. "Why else? I feel like I'm about to throw up and my anxiety is shooting the roof. I wouldn't do this for anyone but Marnie."

Hearing the desperation in my voice, and perhaps taking great amusement at the way I admitted my weaknesses, Mark emitted a high-pitched giggle that no man should ever make. He laid on the floor, laughing into the carpet.

"Eldon? What are you doing?"

I saw Marnie's sneakers as I heard her voice above me. *Shoot. Now I feel like I have to pee. Everyone is walking out of the classroom and I'm just here in the hallway on college campus on all fours.* "Trying to get the girls to stop following me," I said.

"Well, I hate to tell you this, El, but you look even more attractive when you're crawling. You're like a soldier crossing a battlefield. Both of you do."

Oh great, I thought. *Fantastic. But at least she loves my insanity.*

"Marnie," Mark said, "my friend here has been shy and easily embarrassed since I knew him in grade school. Trust me when I say this is the first time I've seen him do anything that ridiculous." He grinned and slapped me on the back when I stood up. "Especially when it comes to avoiding girls."

"Truth," I said.

"And hey," he said, dropping his beloved math book on the floor. He put one arm around me and one arm around Marnie, pulling us close to his face. "Now we got a real epic group here. Fearless. Crazy. Best friends forever."

I groaned at his playful spiel. *Seriously, Mark. Don't get all attached to this arrangement.*

Mark and Geoff knew how I felt about Marnie, but they didn't know the complexities of it or the extent I would go to avoid the pain of a breakup. I wanted more. So much more. But I also wanted to let Marnie be one of the guys if she wanted to. It made things less pressuring. Less daunting. It was good to be platonic. Platonic with a hint of romance.

"And, tell me," Mark said, with a questioning look at Marnie. "Eldon says you know a girl I can go out with. Who is it?"

Marnie gave me a startled but entertained expression, raised eyebrows and all, and she simply said, "Tawny."

Exactly, I thought, sighing out loud. *Marnie, I don't know how but you totally read my mind. Thank goodness.*

"Have I seen her around campus?" Mark asked.

"I don't know. But Eldon is right. She would be your kind of girl."

Mark lifted both his hands to high-five us at the same time, and we obliged. "I am indebted to you, my elvish companions," he said.

Marnie and I watched him swagger away, each of us probably thinking that he was nuts and that we existed in the strangest era of the world. *How is this my life? What kind of people have I bonded with?*

Thirty-Three

Marnie

Friday, October 12th, 2012. 7:35 PM. Arroyo Grande, CA

Eldon and I actually did spend time focused on our school work. We had to. Otherwise we wouldn't have successfully made it to graduation day. But still… much of the days spent together before Thanksgiving was just us hanging out at the bookstore or beach and working on our separate stories and sharing various character and plot ideas.

And we went to see plenty of movies in the theater of course. My favorite memory of movies-at-the-theater with Eldon was the second time we went together. Oh, and I don't remember the names of the movies we saw in the theater. Not a single one.

My sneaky idea of stoking romance involved letting him buy the popcorn and giant drink. One drink. And I said I would get a couple straws for the drink… but I only got ONE straw. *Yes, very clever,* I told myself.

Sitting down in the lower middle portion of the auditorium, I felt nothing but excited chills. Eldon had a hint of a smile when the intro roller coaster animation lit up the screen. Keeping his eyes on the screen and popcorn in hand, he silently leaned one way, and I followed suit, receiving the why-are-they-being-weird looks from people down the row.

Each time there was another turn or drop in the roller coaster animation, we copied it. *I'm trying not to giggle out of sheer childlike joy, but Eldon's serious face is so funny and his being goofy with me is a dream. I have a movie buddy and he doesn't say dumb, critical things. He just enjoys being and living in the present moment like I do. Unadulterated happiness. Pure.* And then at the final moment of the animation, we both hummed the line of dramatic notes, trading smiles as darkness took over the room.

Thirty-Four

Eldon

8:45 PM

I knew Marnie had gotten one straw for our soda and assumed she did want that sort of gross but sweet connection of both our mouths touching it at separate intervals. But that was the least of my concerns during the movie. I struggled in a different area. And fellow men, you know what I mean.

Marnie just HAD to pick that night to wear a dress. A long, classy dress that covered her legs. But a dress. Sitting right next to me. And we still didn't say we were on a date.

Okay, I thought. *I'm totally chill. I'm cool. I'm totally watching the car chase on the screen and not staring at the hot girl I'm falling in love with who is right next to me. The girl who is drinking from the same straw that I'm drinking from.*

I went for the popcorn, subconsciously placing my hand where I thought the bag was, and my chest tightened. Marnie's hand was in the popcorn too. I held my breath as our fingers touched, savoring the feeling of her soft skin against mine. Neither of us looked at each other. We just sat there, our hands in the popcorn bag, holding onto the sensation of each other's touch. *I want to grab her hand so bad,* I thought. *I want to pull her onto my lap and kiss her hair and face and make a big freaking scene in here.*

Marnie was the first to pull away. And I snuck a look at her face. She was trying to hide her grin by taking a long sip of soda. I had to grin too. *Yes. Yes. Yes. Yes.*

Thirty-Five

Marnie

Saturday, October 27th, 2012. 10:28 PM. San Luis Obispo, CA

Eldon had apparently promised Geoff that he'd show up for a Halloween party even though he had tried many times to get out of it. He said it made sense to give in at least once to the request since it was the last Halloween before the end of college. So we both walked down the street from our college campus… wearing our makeshift costumes: Eldon wore his pointy ears, a black shirt that said **"Elvish Superhero"** across the chest, black jeans, and red sneakers. I wore my usual pointy ears, a blue headband with matching blue jeans and shoes, and a pink shirt that said **"I'm With The Elvish Superhero"**. The words were painted on with puffy paint.

And in we walked through the open door of what I thought would be the ultimate drinking-kissing-everything-high fest.

We immediately saw Geoff making out with a random girl on a futon while surrounded by couples and other groups who were engaged in everything that made me blush. The floor was soaked with every color liquid imagined. The combination of booming music, noises that sounded like barn animals, and smells that should be confined to a urinal.

It was… yeah. Pretty much what I expected.

"Um…" Eldon said. He looked at me as I looked up at him. We didn't say it out loud, but I knew we thought the same thing.

Danger zone. Let's get outta here.

"Wanna get ice cream and walk on the beach?" I asked as we ran away.

"You like eating cold food in cold weather too?"

"Yup."

"Let's go."

And believe it or not, there was an ice cream place that was open in the late hours of the night.

Thirty-Six

Eldon

11:45 PM. Cambria, CA

Marnie amazed me the way she deftly handled life as it occurred in all forms of raunchy, scary, and downright perverted. She had her standards. I could always tell. But she was kind and gentle when she spoke about the world. She tried to see the good in everything and in everyone. That alone was a quality that made her a keeper in my mind.

"Sorry, Marnie," I said as we climbed a pile of slippery beach rocks.

"It's okay. I expected that from Geoff. Learned plenty about the way he works."

"No, but I'm sorry that I allowed us to be dragged into that display."

Marnie looked over her shoulder at me. "So, you don't ever drink?"

"Almost never," I said. "I used to smoke and do all the other drug stuff in junior high."

"Really? You don't seem like that type."

"Yeah, well…" I took a breath as I untangled the hair strands from my earring. "Peer pressure got the best of me."

"Then what made you stop?" she asked.

"Well, besides some rotting teeth, I didn't want to destroy my brain before turning twenty. I knew I had book and movie ideas and I didn't want to lose them."

"I'm glad you didn't lose your ideas," Marnie said with a smile.

I was wondering if she was shivering in the ocean air, but I couldn't tell as she continued to walk along the rocks. She balanced herself, keeping her cup of ice cream aloft, and the moonlight suddenly beamed onto us. *Her beautiful red curls,* I thought with a sigh. *So, so beautiful.* "Marn, what are your plans for Thanksgiving? I assume you will be hanging with your family since they live pretty close too."

"No. I'm actually gonna be on my own this year. My parents and sister are traveling to Italy for some extravagant vacation. I don't mind kicking back alone though. I like the quiet."

I felt myself spit out the next sentence so fast. I knew I was being unusually impulsive and stammered in the midst of it. "Would you feel like having Thanksgiving with me?"

There was silence. Dead silence. Just the wind and waves. Marnie stood with her back to me as she breathed slowly.

"Are you going to be with your family?" she asked.

"I am."

"Well, I don't want to intrude on that kind of tradition, Eldon."

Hearing the subtle giddiness in her voice, knowing that she really did want to say yes, I quickly said, "What tradition? It's a bunch of food and sports on TV. I don't have any cousins or extended people. Just my mom, dad, brother, and sisters."

Marnie finally looked at me again, eyes serious. "That's me meeting your family."

Okay, I know this is a lot, I thought. *But it's no big deal. It's not. My family knows from the small bits that I've told them... that we are chill and Marnie is a friend. A best friend. An adorable, sweet, I-could-kiss-her-all-night-long friend. You're talking crazy, El, you know that. Calm down, boyo.*

"My parents were cool with my brother when he invited his friends to holidays in the past. We are pretty much an open door to whoever wants to show up."

Saying that to Marnie, I knew I was fibbing. Not good. I knew it. But she could deal with the overprotective and controlling nature of my mom later. Way later. If my family was to meet and bond with any girl, I wanted it to be with Marnie Staysha Koehn. *My Elf queen.*

"It's your first Thanksgiving alone, Marnie. You said that. You shouldn't have to be alone in your apartment on a special holiday."

Warming up to the idea, Marnie flashed a smile at me as she hopped back onto the sand. "Does that mean I get to see the Christmas tree farm?"

"Of course. My favorite part of visiting my parents is being out among their trees." I was on a roll. I couldn't stop myself. I couldn't stop talking. "And, you know what, you could stay the night there. They have extra rooms in the house."

"What?" Marnie asked with a nervous laugh.

"All right. My bad." I held up my hands, thought for a moment, then ran my fingers tightly through my hair. *Yikes. Think before you talk, Eldon.* "That sounded… sorry. I just meant that every year I stay with them to have that extra time there in the morning too. I hang out with my siblings. My brother especially. We don't see each other much outside of the holidays."

"And your parents know we aren't dating, right? I don't want them thinking or getting their hopes up that we're this intense—"

"No. I promise it's not like that. I can drive us both though if you're good with that. You can bring as many overnight bags as you want. And…I know that came out sounding creepy and weird but I promise I'm not trying to be, Marnie. I'd just really like you to be there with me. Only if you want." I groaned when the words stopped coming and nearly slapped myself in the face.

Marnie was giggling. She reached out and playfully poked my arm, nodding as she said, "I'd love to. What else should we do to make this night more awkward and weird?"

My cheeks were hot with embarrassment, but I was happy that she agreed to my very detailed plan and excruciating explanation. "I think we should just go home now," I said. "Before anymore crazy schemes come out of my mouth."

"You're really cute when you get all worked up and flustered," she said. "And please don't feel stupid, El, because I feel like a complete idiot half the time I'm doing my thing in public."

"But you're never an idiot," I said. I bit my lip, holding back the strongest urge to kiss her. "You're the coolest girl I know."

Thirty-Seven

Marnie

Tuesday, November 6th, 2012. 2:30 PM. San Luis Obispo, CA

At the innocent request of my friend Tawny, I made the decision to check out a writer's group that met in the campus library once a week. I didn't want to do it alone so I asked Eldon if he would go with me since he also loved writing.

"I don't like writer groups," Eldon had said. "They are finicky and critical and there's always some girl who has to be the boss of everyone. And if I walk in with you to see the chairs set up in a circle, I'm gonna give you a signal that I'm annoyed."

"Let's just try it once," I told him. We can use our Vow Of The Silent Kindred to make it fun."

"Okay."

***

We went into the group and there was a circle of chairs. Ten of them. Eight were filled with people who all glanced up from their phones to watch us come in. From the corner of my eye, I saw Eldon gave a stern-faced salute to the ceiling, and I giggled.

"I knew it," he whispered. "Darn chair circle."

"Sooooo," a raven-haired girl in a white sequin shirt said with a sweep of the arm. "What genres do you two write?"

"Fantasy," I said.

"Fantasy with a splash of superhero," Eldon said.

We sat across from each other in the only empty chairs available, Eldon clearly annoyed that he was the only guy in the room, and we had our first "telepathic" conversation with our eyes.

Me: Sorry, El. I didn't know it would be this awkward.

Eldon: No apology necessary. But you need to do something to get us out of here.

Me: Why can't you? I thought you were overcoming your fear of public humiliation.

Eldon: Marnie, please? I HATE this.

I glanced at the floor and saw a crinkly piece of thread. Probably from a shirt that had started to unravel. It sort of looked like a spider. Sort of. The raven-haired girl had begun a tedious monologue, reading aloud from what looked to be an hour long story of her own creation. She liked to hear herself talk. And everyone else had their heads down on their tablets and phones. No one wanted to admit that she was boring and too I'm-in-charge-so-you-have-to-listen-to-me for the writer group.

All right, I thought. *Time for a dumb idea.* "Spider!" I shrieked. "Oh my gosh! Eldon, kill it!"

He jumped up with me, stomped on the thread, and we sprinted out of the room. All eyes were on us. I heard the raven-haired girl call out in a pissed off nasally voice, "Are you freaking kidding me?"

Tears ran down my face as I laughed. I grabbed onto Eldon to keep from falling down, and he lightly gripped my arm as he chuckled. I think he chuckled more at my overzealous reaction than the stupid distraction itself, but it was cute.

"I guess it's not that funny," I said, wiping my eyes.

"Oh, you are funny," he said. "You're such a lively, wonder-eyed spitfire, Marnie. A total ball of relentless energy."

It was funny to hear him speak so calmly as I was still a giggly mess. We went out of the building and I felt Eldon wrap his arms around my waist, gently hugging me from behind. He didn't say a word as he held me. Then he let go and walked past me as if nothing had happened. *Adorable. Darn freakin adorable.*

Thirty-Eight

Eldon

Thursday, November 22nd, 2012. 1:50 PM

Thanksgiving. On the road to Atascadero to spend the day and night with my family. And with Marnie. My best friend who couldn't have been hotter or driven me wilder than she did with her playful brown eyes. Nervous wasn't the word. I was petrified of introducing her to my clan.

"Do you mind if I give you a rundown of everything?" I asked.

Marnie was so casual and relaxed next to me. She worked on her laptop, chewing the peppermint gum I gave her, and looked out the window as I drove. "You mean you wanna tell me all the little things I should know before walking into the Cornade household?"

"Yes. Now, this is very important…" I began talking so fast and so out of order and context that I wasn't sure if I made any sense. But Marnie just let me talk. Which honestly was very nice of her.

"A weird thing about my parents. I don't often call them 'Mom' or 'Dad'. Years ago my brother and I crafted names that were more fantasy-like for them and surprisingly they think it's sweet. So we go with that."

"So, what do you call them?"

"Mom is 'Arda'. Dad is 'Bridge'. You can call them that too."

"That's really epic, Eldon."

Epic. I started to smile, but the nerves took over again.

"Question," Marnie said. "How nervous would you be if I was actually your girlfriend?"

"Oh, I'd be a disaster. Complete loss of coordination or words."

"Why?"

"What do you mean?" I asked. "You're not nervous?"

"A little. But it's not like we're announcing our love or engagement to them. We're friends."

"Super close friends," I said. "You're still cool with staying the night, right?"

"Sure." Marnie said it with total calm in her voice. She was furiously deleting a sentence she had just typed.

"My younger sisters have their own rooms," I went on. "They are twins by the way. Fifteen years old. And I think you'll be in the library. I'll be in the guest room."

"And your brother?"

"Couch. He always takes the couch." *Darn it. Made a wrong turn.*

"El, you know I'm totally chill about it all, right?"

"Yeah." I made sure I was driving in the right direction again before talking more about my family. I got so, so carried away with details. It was dumb. "My brother's name is Hendrix. He has a strange black cat that acts like a dog that he always walks around on a harness."

"What is the cat's name?"

"Manly."

"What are your sisters' names?"

"Lonnie and Talitha. They might bug you a lot. Lotta questions or try to make you feel like an outcast in the house."

"I'm used to that. What else?"

"Um… my mom is very—"

"You mean Arda?" Marnie said.

I quickly looked at her, seeing her mischievous smile. I smiled back. More relaxed. She calmed me down. "Yeah. Arda. She's a very strong, loud personality."

"I know. You gave me that hint already. I'll be fine."

"Okay. If you feel uncomfortable about anything just tell me. But I don't know if I'll be able to remedy it. Because, you know, I end up feeling like a kid around my family. They sort of steal my thunder."

"Families can do that sometimes. I know you're not shy or awkward, El."

"No, I am. You just bring out the other side, Marnie. It's amazing actually. I feel like a different man when I'm with you. More free-spirited. Accepted."

We traded smiles as she said, "You're welcome, Jaeger."

Thanks for coming with me, Arrowswan, I thought. *I really need your emotional support. I don't wanna seem crazy. But you help me. You help me a lot.*

"That intense, huh?" Marnie says knowingly.

"Well, if you can handle Geoff and Mark and their antics, you can handle my family." I loosened my grip on the wheel as we pulled into my parents' driveway. "Promise."

Thirty-Nine

Marnie

2:40 PM

Surrounded by trees. I drew in a deep breath as I spun around in the dirt, not caring who was watching me dance. Christmas trees equaled magic. I felt honored to be at my best friend's Christmas tree farm on Thanksgiving day.

"Baby boy!" screeched an immaculately dressed woman to our left. She ran awkwardly toward us in her high heels and dress, not at all looking like a pro at the whole fancy-style gig. I had to figure that she was just dressed up for the holiday.

"Hi, Arda," Eldon said with a smile. He gently embraced her while she squeezed him hard.

His mom, I thought. *Of course. Whew. Close to getting one introduction out of the way.*

"C'mere, baby," Arda said, dragging Eldon away from the van. "Look what your dad got for his collection."

I stood there alone. Unsure. Yet... not surprised. *Of course this woman would ignore me. And Eldon is so being babied right now. Dude. He is about to turn twenty-four. Not ten.*

"Are you Marnie?"

I looked to who said my name. The guy was close to Eldon's height, but his hair was a dark brown and very short and spiky.

"Yeah," I said.

He smiled. "I'm Hendrix."

I smiled back. *Eldon's big brother. Good looking guy too.*

"So, you're getting the whole family introduction today, huh?"

"I guess," I said.

"Don't be intimidated by the parents. I promise we aren't all as fussy over El as they are."

"What made them get like that?"

Hendrix chuckled as he bent to study a tree. "You'd think as his older brother I'd have more insight, but I really don't. Let's just say he was one of those kids who needed an extra push to grow up."

"Well, I think he's awesome," I said. "Really awesome."

"I see that, Marnie. Boyfriend and girlfriend."

"No. We're not dating. We're just hanging out."

"Hanging out." Hendrix grinned and shook his head. "We'll see how long that lasts." He suddenly gave a low whistle and a black cat came running and jumped up onto his shoulder.

I giggled and asked, "Is this Manly?"

"Yeah. You can pet him. He's super chill."

After giving Manly the cat a quick pet, I turned to the house. "Hopefully your parents won't mind my company. I mostly took up Eldon's invite because my own family is out of town."

"Yeah, no worries, Marnie. We're all cool." Hendrix motioned for me to follow him. "C'mon. I think a lot of the food is ready."

"You don't eat later?"

"My dad has always orchestrated the eating times for holidays. Usually on Thanksgiving it's chowing down at three or three-thirty and then we all just sit around with whatever sports are on TV."

I smiled at the upbeat energy in his voice. At least he was making me feel at home.

* * *

When I walked into the house and silently sat next to Eldon at his mom's beloved cherry wood table, I felt the attention turn onto me. The prodding stares of his sisters, brother, and his mom and dad. It made me feel like I was sitting on a do-not-touch-that shelf display and I was a crystal object about to tip over.

Eldon had the least amount of food of anyone on his plate. While I gladly took a decent serving of every dish that I saw, Eldon had only a small bit of turkey, mashed potatoes, and green bean casserole. He didn't smile much as he ate next to me. Didn't seem comfortable.

His parents mostly talked with Hendrix, asking about his girlfriend and where she was currently and about his job as a high school geography teacher. I learned that Hendrix was thirty years old.

"So, Eldon," Arda asked in a startlingly shrill voice, "you still excited about the editor assistant job in New York?"

I felt like a bomb had just been dropped on my head. *Eldon's leaving? When?* "You're going to New York?" I asked him.

"Not excited," he said to his mom. And to me he said, "Yeah. New York City. Right after graduation. Hadn't gotten to telling you that detail yet, but that's the job I was talking about when we first had coffee together."

Several long trains of thought collided as I realized what that meant. What that meant for our friendship and for a possible future as a serious couple. It meant an end. It wasn't going to work.

But... no. No. It's not gonna be bad. It will be okay, Marnie, I told myself. *Just act normal. You're not having a meltdown right now. You're not panicking at all.* "Oh," I said, clutching my fork tightly as if I could manipulate it like a stress ball. "That's cool. Just for the summer or what?"

"He is moving there. Permanently," Arda said.

The smirk on her face. Why is she looking at him like that? How can a mother be so pushy to her son?

"No. A year. I may not like it."

"We agreed you would stay with the company for as long as you can. You'll have time on weekends to write your scripts."

"Screenplays," Eldon said tensely. His eyebrows were furrowed and he didn't stop clearing his throat.

"What's up, El?" his dad Bridge asked. "You're not into New York anymore?"

I don't think he ever was, I thought to myself. *The tension at this table though. My goodness. You would need a butcher knife to slice through it.* I traded sympathetic looks with Hendrix who was watching Eldon from across the table. Both of their sisters, Lonnie and Talitha, were busy texting. *Figures,* I thought. *Teens in their own world. Totally disconnected.*

"He doesn't wanna be behind the scenes pushing papers. He wants to be in the spotlight." Arda spoke with a harsh, mocking tone, and I could see Eldon getting absolutely agitated. But he said nothing.

If he won't rise up against the tyranny then I will. "Writing screenplays is also kind of behind the scenes," I said. "It's a balance. I think a lot of us want to see our name in lights."

They all looked at me. *Yikes.* I shocked myself in standing up for him and was trembling as I reached for my wine glass, trembling so much that Hendrix kindly held the bottom of it for me so I could pour more wine.

"So, you're dating a spitfire," Arda said with a sharp look to Eldon.

"Mom," he said, "we are not dating. And Marnie's very easy-going. She is the most chill girl I've had as a friend."

Okay. I love hearing that but when will the tension die down? At this rate me and Hendrix will be finishing off the wine and I'll be asking for some harder alcohol.

"That's great, El," Bridge said loudly. It was obvious at that point that he was trying to shut his wife's coarseness off. "What's your major, Marnie?" he asked me.

"Comm Studies," I said.

Eldon smiled at me. "Yeah, but she is a writer too. Published author and everything. Taking the book world by storm."

I smiled back, feeling him lay his hand on my knee under the table.

"Definitely am working on it," I said to anyone who cared to listen.

His parents and siblings didn't say or ask much else of me. They preferred to whisper and gossip among themselves as they drifted to the TV in the living room. An ice hockey game happened to be on and I sat with Eldon and Hendrix on the couch to watch with them.

Eldon put his hand on my leg, I thought. Sneakily. I could feel his fingers starting to rub down my knee when he did that. *Darn nuggets... so hard to stay in the platonic zone. Goosebumps everywhere.*

"Hey, Marnie, can you help us with something?"

I looked back to where Eldon's twin sisters were huddled with their phones. They had matching straight blonde hair and fuzzy pink jackets and boots. "What?" I asked.

"Can you come here?" Lonnie said, waving me over.

I gave a look to Eldon who shrugged and half-smiled. "Just see what they want," he said quietly. "I think they just wanna have girl talk."

"I'm sure," I said back. I left the couch and followed Lonnie and Talitha out the front door of the house.

"What's up?" I asked.

"So, I don't know if you know this about Eldon, Marnie, but he laughs really hard at ducks."

"Ducks? Like real ducks?"

Talitha giggled, holding her phone up as she said, "No! Rubber toy ducks! We used to do this prank like five years ago and he thought it was the funniest thing and we wanna do it again. You need to see how hard he laughs at it."

"Literally," Lonnie said. "Soda shoots out his nose and he falls over. Will you do it?"

"Well, what's the prank?"

"We're filling his van with yellow rubber ducks."

Okay. That sounds fun. The lowkey prankster in me wanted to play along. "I'm with you," I said excitedly. "Where do we get the ducks?"

"Over there," Talitha said. "We gotta move 'em from the shed to his van."

Game face. I could hear an epic superhero theme play in my head as I followed his sisters. I was such a hyper dork. Felt like prepping for battle. "And how did you get his keys?"

"Oh, please," Lonnie said with a pretend evil laugh, "we have our ways."

Forty

Eldon

5:20 PM

"What do you think the girls are doing?" I asked Hendrix.

"Probably something dumb."

I glanced out the window but didn't see anyone. "They've been gone awhile. Really quiet."

"Maybe they're bonding with your not-girlfriend-girlfriend."

"Not now," I said, throwing an ice chip at him. "Stop."

"Why you all shy about Marnie? You're being hot and cold with her."

"No. We just don't want to rush anything, Hendrix."

"El," he said, turning his back on the TV in a manner which I never saw him do before, "don't let that whole 'I'm-not-cool-enough-to-get-a-girl' thing trip you up. Marnie seems like a really amazing girl. A woman in all respects."

"I can't start dating someone when I'm leaving in June. If we start kissing and tempted to do all the rest of it… it'll mess me up forever. I don't want to ruin the vision I have of her."

Hendrix fell back on the couch and shook his head as I kept eating ice chips. "There is no vision!" he said, raising his arms to the ceiling. "She's in front of you! If you like her make it real. Or she'll be gone. Some other guy will snap her up in a year or two guaranteed if you don't."

I couldn't look directly in my brother's eyes. He thought he knew my heart. My parents thought they knew what was best for my future. It was maddening. Hurtful. But I never wanted them to know that they were winning against me. I was supposed to be a strong man who didn't break down over worrying he would lose the possible love of his life.

"If she's the one I'll know it," I said.

"When?" Hendrix asked.

"When it's time."

* * *

The silence between us turned awkward and remained so for a few more minutes as the game kept going on the TV. All at once we heard the front door slam and Lonnie ran in with wide eyes.

"Eldon! Someone broke into your van!"

"What?" I jumped off the couch and Hendrix flew up with me, spilling his jar of peanuts everywhere. "Are they out there? What'd they steal?"

I ran so fast, my shoes sliding in the mud as I saw Marnie outside with Talitha. They opened the doors to my van and a flood of yellow rubber ducks poured out.

"What the hedge?" Hendrix shouted next to me. "Again?"

And I died. I died laughing.

To this day I can't fully explain why yellow rubber ducks make me laugh so much, but I tell you what… Marnie and my sisters got me good that day. Because I did in fact run outside holding a can of soda, and although I didn't laugh it out my nose, Hendrix spit his beer all over the ground when we saw a second stream of yellow ducks come flying out the back of the van. Tumbling out with such speed that it looked like someone had turned on a magical faucet of a rubber duck bathtub.

I couldn't breathe. I couldn't stay standing. I stumbled forward in my unmanly giggling, trying to reach Marnie to give her a little shove or tickle or anything to show playful revenge. By the time my parents came out to see what was so funny, we all, sisters and Marnie included, had terribly sore stomachs and ribs from laughing so hard.

Again, please, don't judge me on this. I don't know why I found it and still find it so hysterical. It just was. It was the highlight of that Thanksgiving. Well, besides seeing Marnie with messy hair and in her pajamas…

Forty-One

Marnie

11:10 PM

I was completely fine with sleeping in the library. It took awhile for me to lay down as I looked through the Cornade bookshelves, but eventually I did climb into the perfectly-sized Murphy bed. I found myself itching to tell someone about my day with Eldon and called Tawny. Literally talking to her on the phone under the covers.

Yeah. I was weird.

"Hey. Tawny. Can you hear me?"

"Marnie? Why are you whispering?"

"I'm at Eldon's family's house," I said.

"What? Why are you calling me to say that? We aren't sixteen anymore."

"I know, but I have to tell you something else."

"What is it?"

I could tell by the energy in her voice that she was fully awake. Probably was at some party.

"I think I'm falling in love," I said.

"Um, Marnie, you would say that about any guy with long blond hair."

"No."

"Yes. You would. C'mon, girl. Don't deny it."

I sighed, wanting to debate her on the subject, but also didn't want to raise my voice. If I was caught like this: talking about a guy while under the covers at his parents' house… it would be more than embarrassing.

"Okay. Forget it. I gotta go."

"Wait, wait! Marn, did you see what he's wearing?"

I rolled my eyes when I heard the grin in her voice. "No, I didn't see his pajamas," I said.

"My gosh, girl. What if he sleeps in nothing? You should totally sneak in his room and—"

Oh no. I ended the call when I heard a knock. I threw the covers off, made sure my pajama top and leggings were covering everything, and went to open the door.

"What?" I called out as I stood against it. I sincerely hoped it wasn't Eldon's mom come to give me a critical lecture about my dream job.

"It's me, Marn. You good?"

I bit my lip before opening the door. Eldon stood in front of me, long blond hair all messy, wearing the cutest long sleeve shirt with an astronaut on it and matching space pajama bottoms.

Forty-Two

Eldon

11:34 PM

I knew it probably looked bad the way I came to Marnie's door in the middle of the night, but I honestly couldn't get her out of my head as I was laying down in the guest room. She had experienced a lot of overwhelming interactions with my family and I had to make sure she was okay.

Her messy curls over her eyes. The tight pink shirt and blue leggings. Wow. So, so magnificent. Cue the rockin' 80s ballad.

"I just wanted to be sure you were… warm enough. It can be drafty in this house. Old walls and cracks and stuff."

A small smile lit her face as she watched me grow sheepish. "I'm fine, Eldon."

"Do you need anything in the morning? Anything special for breakfast?"

"Long as I'm able to get a second breakfast," she said with a wink.

Second breakfast. Of course. Reference from our favorite movie. From The Lord Of The Rings. Yet… there are such filthy meanings that could be taken out of that phrase. Darn it, boyo. Keep your mind clean. Cheez. I breathed out hard as a chill shot up my spine. "Yeah. Like we have lots of cinnamon rolls probably. Or muffins. I remember you like muffins like you had that one at the coffee place."

"Yes." She laughed softly. "I love sweet things."

I nodded, hating myself for sounding like a bumbling idiot. *Why do I sometimes sound calm and confident and other times I can't talk without stammering? She drives me crazy.*

"Okay. Hope you sleep good. Sorry if I woke you up."

"You didn't," she said.

I backed away, hearing her close the door, and I pulled my phone from my pocket. I hate texting with a vengeance, but I wanted one of my buddies to know. And it was so out of character for me to gossip. It really was.

Text To Mark: HEY. SRRY TO BE WEIRD BUT I HAVE TO TELL U SOMETHING BOUT MARNIE

Text From Mark: WHATS UP? I DIDNT HIT IT OFF WITH HER FRIEND BTW BUT AGREED MARNIE IS COOLEST GIRL WE KNOW

What? We?! It was illogical, but I got worried. I freaked out. I thought that maybe since Mark was a cool, fun guy that he had a shot with her too. That maybe he would try to get her attention. I wanted to do anything to stay in Marnie's center sights.

I need to tell her my feelings without telling her. She knows I think she is cute and sweet. But I need to do something else. I need to make a loving gesture.

Forty-Three

Marnie

Friday, November 23rd, 2012. 7:01 AM

I woke up to Eldon right outside the door again. This time, he came holding a hot cup of coffee. He held it out to me with a shy, close-mouthed smile.

"I didn't tell you to do this for me," I said.

"Well, I wanted to. You've mentioned that you're a grouchy goblin in the morning without your coffee. I had to remedy that."

I didn't remember when I had told him such a fact, but I loved that he brought me coffee. It was friend-mantic. "Thanks, Jaeger."

"You're welcome, Arrowswan," he said.

"Are we hanging out here for awhile after breakfast?" I asked.

"Not too much. We should get back to our private corners, wouldn't you say? Family's driving me a little nuts."

I chuckled and sipped the coffee. "A little."

7:18 AM

While enjoying the view of Eldon at the kitchen counter happily drinking his coffee loaded with creamer, I spontaneously decided I wanted to eat sweet potatoes and green bean casserole for breakfast along with my cinnamon roll. So I put them in the microwave.

"Fun fact, Marnie," Eldon said, gesturing to me with his mug, "I hate microwaves. Food should always be warmed up on a stove or in a real oven."

The seriousness on his face tickled me. "Okay," I said. "But I have to say that I like them for heating things in a rush."

"But it gets all mushy then."

"So what?"

"Marn, really? That's not cool."

"Why? Microwaves won't kill you. It's not like they are robots."

"Oh," he said firmly, "they are robots."

What is he getting so worked up for? I bit back a smile when he got up and came over to me in his adorable pajamas, his long hair all askew. He waited for me to take my plate out of the microwave and looked at it and then at me.

"Wanna explain your actions, Elf queen?" he asked in a dramatic voice.

I didn't know if he was kidding or not. I just stood, looking back at him. I had to lift my head to meet his eyes, and I felt squirmy and sexy standing barefoot with him in his family's kitchen. Both in our pajamas. Both looking like we had just had a long night of hay rolling.

Then he laughed.

I laughed.

And then Eldon playfully grabbed me around the waist, tickling me to the point where I had to set my food down or I would have spilled it everywhere.

"Our first debate," he said in the midst of tickle-attacking me, "was about microwaves."

Microwaves, I thought. *So random. So perfectly random. I love goofing around with Eldon.*

I appreciated that first holiday with him in his family's house. I appreciated it so, so much. More than he realized.

Forty-Four

Eldon

Saturday, December 8th, 2012. 7:20 PM

I gestured to the back seat at a red gift bag when Marnie climbed in. We were going to drive to see Christmas Light Row and I made sure to bring a present for her since she had just turned twenty-three on the sixth.

"Happy birthday, Arrowswan," I said. "Rule number eight from Geoff's guide to dating: getting a gift for the girl's birthday or Christmas, especially early on, choose something under thirty bucks or they will think they owe you. But make sure it's still something they would use or wear. PS: Don't add to the junk in their purse."

Marnie laughed as she pulled the tissue paper out. "Did Geoff really invent a guidebook?"

"He did," I said. "Weird, I know."

"Not really. He's girl crazy."

"True. And I know we still aren't dating. But I figured I should add to the cute accessories you always wear."

Marnie squealed in excitement when she pulled out the dangly narwhal earrings. "They are adorable! And good news, Jaeger. I got something for you too since your birthday is tomorrow."

"Yeah?" I glanced down at what she was taking out of her purse.

"Here."

It was a t-shirt that said: **"King Of The Elves"**. *Sweet Marnie. She so gets me.*

"I love that," I said. "Thank you."

"So, tell me if this is crazy," Marnie said, looking out the window. "Feel like walking it?"

"Walking among the lights?"

"Yeah."

"Sure," I said. *Way to go all romance novel on me, Elf queen.*

Forty-Five

Marnie

8:05 PM. San Luis Obispo, CA

"I love that sweater on you, Marnie."

"Thanks." I noticed Eldon push his hands further into his jean pockets as we walked to the next street. "Yours is nice too."

"I don't normally wear bulky sweaters like this but thought I should go with the theme of the night."

"Theme of the night?" I asked with a chuckle.

"Well, you with your light-up reindeer earrings and the goofy fireplace Christmas sweater. I had to represent with my own holiday spirit." He motioned to himself and dramatically spun around on the sidewalk. "Me in my ugly burnt marshmallow brown sweater."

"Yes," I said. "It's very cute. Kinda like a dorky dad."

"Dorky dad," Eldon echoed. "Really? You see me as a dorky dad?"

"Oh, I see you as a great dad for any kid, El."

I saw him silently grinning and I felt warm inside as we watched groups of little kids scampering around us. There was a Santa Claus riding up and down the neighborhood streets on top of a fire truck, creating a magical, cheerful vibe for everyone who was out to see the Christmas lights. So many smiles and laughter and candy canes being passed out by families standing outside their homes.

And Eldon's hairstyle tonight. My word. Oooh. He had put some of his long hair in a topknot and let the rest fall down his back with a few tiny braids tucked behind his left ear. Like a rugged Norse Viking or samurai.

"Hey, look."

I followed Eldon, seeing where he was pointing. A family had set up a makeshift theater screen right in front of their house and was playing *The Polar Express.* "My favorite part," he said, looking completely enchanted by it.

"Oh yeah. The train tracks turning into a roller coaster ride. That is a cool part."

"So cool," Eldon said.

"It is." I looked up at his eyes, seeing him gaze down at me. He always felt taller when we were this close. My arm was pressed against his. "It's cute that you like it, El."

Forty-Six

Eldon

8:23 PM

Marnie's adorable face. The way she's looking at the kids out here. And how she already has a name for a future son. Halfdan. Aww. I'll never forget that. So cute. I want to continue traditions with her. I want us to form traditions together of our own.

It felt like love. It really did. But that feeling terrified me. It made me feel like throwing up. It was the best and worst sensations all tangled like a clump of copper wire in my chest. My heart felt like it was beating for her...

Christmas itself was very mellow for us. We celebrated separately with our own families, trying to ease back on close hanging out time for a while. Mostly to get more studying done.

Forty-Seven

Marnie

From January to May there were only a couple memories worthy of being written down. Between the serious but epic weekly writing sessions at the bookstore and our days of goofing off at the antique store, we had so much fun making the most of what time we had before Eldon left for New York.

1. Eldon doing an awful impersonation of Elvis but being so hot in his blue leather jacket and shiny boots that allowed him to skid across the floor.
2. And me trying to moonwalk in roller skates while holding a bottle of hard lemonade… slamming into a shelf full of old plush animals. (Luckily they weren't plates or glass ornaments.) All the animals rained onto my head and Eldon spit out ginger ale in his laughter.
3. Our impromptu staring contest that we did while in the bookstore. We sat in different corners of the store, working on our own stories, and I decided to hold my gaze as Eldon looked at me with the cap of his pen in his mouth. We were so dorky. His blue eyes

were so wide. I lost that contest.

4. And I did publish *Arrowswan* in the final weeks of January. Began writing the sequel in March.

We never kissed. We wanted to. But we didn't. I could feel myself more intensely bonded to him as we approached our graduation day, and I was afraid of how my body and mind would react when he had to leave.

I don't want to lose my best friend. I don't want to lose my Eldon.

Forty-Eight

Eldon

Friday, May 31st, 2013. 9:21 AM. San Luis Obispo, CA

Graduation day. So many nerves. Confused. I don't want to leave tomorrow. I really don't want to leave.

"You ready to do this?" Mark asked me. He was bouncing like a kid in his cap and gown, not seeming like a serious math geek.

"I guess."

"What's up? It's Marnie, isn't it? You don't wanna leave her tomorrow."

"Of course I don't," I said.

Mark waved past me at Geoff who was wildly charging toward us. "Just don't go to New York," he said. "Stay here. Write your screenplays."

I started to tell him why I couldn't back out of the move, but Geoff roughly slapped my back and yelled in my ear, "Yo, dudes! This is it!"

"Someone had a few early drinks," I mumbled.

"Or smokes," Mark said, giving Geoff a light punch on the arm.

"Hey, Eldon!" Geoff said way too loudly, "where's your girl at?"

"Can you calm yourself? She's over there talking with her dancer

133

friends."

"Ohh yeah!" Mark called gleefully. "The guys who you hate because they can dance as good as her!"

"Shut up, Mark," I said.

"No, I'm right. Hey, Geoff, you go get in line and we'll be right there."

I was confused as Mark grabbed my arm and led me to a less-bustling corner of the campus. "What?" I asked.

"I gotta be honest about something, El," he said. "You know how I've been doing the whole math teacher or mathematician thing?"

"Yeah."

"Well…"

"What?" I asked. "What do you want?"

"I'm going to film school. Right after this."

Wow, I thought. *A little jealous but excited for him.* "But why? Why now? I thought you were the numbers guy."

Mark squinted at me. "You don't remember, Eldon? I loved pretending to make movies when we were kids. We both did."

"Yeah." I nodded. "Yeah, I do remember that."

"I always wanted to do my own movies. The independent route. But I'm going to learn what I can as I build my own company."

I didn't fully believe that he would see that plan through, but I smiled. *Annoying that I can't pursue my dream job without my parents making me feel guilty.* "But why are you telling me about this now, Mark? Why are we talking away from everyone else?"

"Because I don't wanna jinx it. You know how things go. I trust you the most because you want to write movies too. And…"

"Yeah?"

"Well," he said, "I'll reach out to you if I need any screenplays. Promise you'll keep in touch?"

"Of course I will. We're buddies."

We did some stupid, dorky handshake (Mark's idea. Not mine.) that we hadn't done since junior high, laughing as we failed to remember the order of movements.

Getting my degree didn't feel real. It was a few hours of spacing out into my world of Jaeger Bowen while names were continuously called. All in slow motion.

My life would change forever once I crossed that stage. It was strange.

Forty-Nine

Marnie

Saturday, June 1st, 2013. 6:45 AM

Convincing Eldon to let me drive him to the airport wasn't that hard. I saw how anxious he was. He kept fumbling with his luggage and running his hands through his hair.

It's gonna be fine. We gotta do this, I told myself. I stood with him, looking to where he needed to go next. The dreaded security line.

"Eldon?" I said quietly, bracing for an unpleasant response.

"Yeah?" he said. He was looking at all the signs in the terminal.

"Have you thought about kissing?"

"Yeah. I think about kissing."

"Do you think about kissing certain girls?"

"All the time."

"I have this fantasy—" I started to say.

"Well, maybe you should keep that fantasy secret."

My heart dropped when Eldon said that. I crossed my arms across my chest, blowing out a shaky breath. "You don't ever feel like kissing me?"

"I don't wanna worry about breaking up, Marnie. I don't wanna be forced to make that decision."

"I know." I studied a dark spot on the white floor. "Better to be friends."

"Yeah. But I'm excited for your future. You'll just keep getting bigger and bigger until one day there won't be a single shelf in the world without a copy of your bestselling books."

I tried to smile, but tears stopped my effort, and I turned away from him. "You're being too optimistic, Eldon."

"I'm being honest." He laid his hand on my shoulder, squeezed it, and embraced me from behind. "I'm going to miss you so much, Marnie."

I faced him once I'd wiped the tears from my cheeks. "I'll miss you too."

Eldon tilted his head as he noticed me falling apart in front of him. "You gonna be okay?"

"Yeah." I sniffed hard, embarrassed that I couldn't keep from crying. "I'll listen to some eighties ballads on the drive back."

"Keep dancing like you always do. Everyone else needs your joyful, sweet light." He surprised me with a very romantic gesture, winding his fingers in my hair, pulling my face close to his, and touched his forehead to mine. "You got this, Arrowswan," he whispered. "You got this."

"I'll see you on the other side, Jaeger," I whispered back to him.

We stepped back from each other after another embrace, staring in each other's eyes, and we nodded at the same time, turning our backs as we went our separate ways. I could hear him walking faster and faster with his wheelie bag. But I only moved forward a few steps before I froze and breathed in as deep as I could without tearing up again.

If he's meant to be mine he will come back. But he might like the city. He might find a better girl there. God, please help me move on if he isn't for me.

But what if I love him? NO. Stop, Marnie. You'll be fine. Someone else will come around. It'll be a God thing.

But I could picture Eldon running back to me. I could picture him spinning me around, kissing me, and the noises in the airport would all fade away. It would just be us.

Fifty

Eldon

8:30 AM

I sat down, watching everyone around me as they settled in for the flight. All I could think about was Marnie and how she should be next to me. I could've asked her to come with. *She's probably still waiting out there. She might even come sprinting down the runway barefoot with her wild red hair in the wind. So gorgeous. Dorky. My Arrowswan.* I never made a declaration of love because I didn't want to jinx us. I should have. In the minute of our goodbye hug, I should have given her the most epic kiss. But if I had kissed her I doubt I would have gotten on the plane.

But maybe she'll move on tomorrow. Maybe she'll forget about me.

* * *

6:30 PM. New York City, NY

You know that feeling where you feel more alone in a crowd than standing by yourself? That's what I was thinking when I stepped out of that airport. I was among hundreds, thousands, yet I felt lost without Marnie next to me. I didn't know for absolute certainty that she was my other half until that moment. She wasn't there to dance spontaneously under the bright lights or whisper off-the-wall observations and giggle with me.

It wasn't just a want. It was a need. I craved being near her.

The confidence I had gained while bonding with her dropped the minute I was engulfed by my new environment. I was scared. Shaking. I knew I had made a mistake. But I didn't want to tell anyone.

Fifty-One

Marnie

Most of the summer passed by without any great incident. Both of us tried to keep our minds on our jobs with Eldon doing his best to figure out the whole corporate thing and city people vibe, and me working odd jobs like walking dogs, tutoring kids in reading, randomly winning a song lyric contest and getting a few hundred bucks out of it, and of course, quietly publishing my sequel to *Arrowswan*.

I also spent a lot of time lying in the sand at the beach and the floor of my apartment listening to Enya and being sad. The Enya songs I played the most on repeat were "Lothlorien" and "Caribbean Blue". It helped me work through the raging emotions.

Since Eldon hated texting and I hated talking on the phone, we didn't communicate often. I knew we were both trying to imagine a life without the other, and we were trying to ignore the miserable I-miss-my-best-friend pains. But the last week of August was different. That's when I got a text from Eldon that I didn't think I'd see.

Text From Eldon: HEY MARNIE. I KNOW YOU HATE TALKING ON THE PHONE BUT WILL YOU PLEASE CALL ME? I WANNA

HEAR YOUR VOICE. I MISS YOU. ALSO I HAVE THE MOST ANNOYING ROOMMATES...WORSE THAN YOU KNOW WHO.

Fifty-Two

Eldon

Saturday, August 31st, 2013. 3:31 PM. New York City, NY

I knew that the text I sent sounded super forward and a little desperate. But I did miss Marnie, and even though she was probably trying to play it cool, I had to believe that deep down she was dying to talk to me too. She always had the most fun, random things to say.

Been so long since we talked. Longer than I want to go without talking again.

I got some amused looks from the triplet brothers when I literally jumped up at the sound of my phone ringing. Those guys were always playing obnoxious opera music and rehearsing scenes for various commercials and Broadway productions. It had gotten very old but I could only afford to live in a shared space like before.

"Hi, Marnie. How are you doing?"

"I'm okay," she said. "How's the city?"

I went to the window as I held the phone to my ear, thinking about sitting on the fire escape. "It's not as nice as being near the coast."

"Well, yeah, but you got a coast there too," she said.

"True." I glanced over my shoulder when I heard one of the guys, Anton, make a crude joke about me and Marnie. I frowned at him and went out on the fire escape, looking out at the sea of buildings. Brown. Grey. Metal. So cold. Not magical at all.

"I'm going to do a book signing here at the store, Eldon," Marnie said.

"Oh yeah?"

"Yeah."

I could tell she really wanted me to pay attention to the tone of her voice. I had to block out the sounds of honking and cursing in the streets as I listened to what she said.

"December seventh. It's a Saturday. Would you be able to come for it?"

"This year, right?" I asked.

"Yes. This coming December."

"I don't know, Marn." I closed my eyes as I forced the words out. "I don't plan on coming back that way for awhile. I wanted to try to at least spend a full year here without going anywhere else."

"Did you promise your mom that?" Marnie asked. Her voice was tight. She sounded like she was holding back tears.

"Well, yeah. I mean… you know. Sort of, yes. But it's just that I need to…"

Marnie sighed on the other end and I felt her exasperation in my bones. The pain and restrained anger she was harboring toward my parents. *Maybe mad at me too. I don't blame her. I'm a coward.* "I don't know, Marnie," I said. "But you know I miss you, right?"

"Yep, I do. Well, if you end up hooking up with someone else, promise you won't tell me. Just do what you have to do."

Oh no. She's pushing me away. I groaned into the phone as I said, "I'm not going to. I don't like any of these girls in my office. None of them are as awesome as you."

"But we aren't together," Marnie said. Her tone was almost fiery. "You can do what you want, okay? I'll be fine. I have to go. Gonna go write at the bookstore. Bye, Eldon."

She hung up before I could say goodbye back to her. The anger that came from her mouth came from a place of heartache. I knew that. I knew that so well. And as I turned to go back inside the apartment, I felt guilty knowing that as soon as Marnie hung up the phone she had started to cry.

"How's your girl?" Anton asked from his shirtless handstand in the middle of the living room. He was smirking at me. "Broken heart, huh?"

"Yeah. I wish I could just go be with her."

"Then do it. You're so afraid to be your own man, El."

"I'm not afraid when I'm with her," I said. "She's incredible." And I began telling Anton all about her sexy dance moves. "I wish I could dance. We could be that musically inclined power couple."

Anton looked from me in my moping state to his brothers who were drinking "healthy" fruit smoothies at the kitchen counter. Lenny and Otto went to the old school stereo that was positioned next to the TV and they caught my eye before turning it on.

"Whoa!" I said, sliding off the couch. "Turn it down, dudes."

"Not until you show us some dancing, man. C'mon. Do it. Do it for your girl."

"I can't."

"I think you can," Anton said. He slapped my shoulder and got down into a breakdancing routine.

The downstairs neighbors are gonna hate us, I thought. "We're going to break something."

"Exactly. I'll show you how to do it, El. C'mon! Do something crazy. All you do is get home from your office job and sit around here watching *The Lord Of The Rings* on repeat."

I watched the triplet brothers show off moves that were much too intense to contain inside the apartment walls. The songs changed from hip hop to rap to pop and then techno. I sat there for hours. Thinking about Marnie.

"For you, baby," I suddenly whispered at eleven o'clock at night. I heard the emotion in my own voice and it struck me what I needed. "I want you to be mine."

And I started moving like how I saw the guys. Then I started throwing my own style in. I sucked. I really sucked at dancing and staying on beat. But I made up my mind that everyone in my office building would know that I was taken. That I had a girlfriend back home.

Girlfriend, I thought to myself. *Marnie IS my girlfriend. I'm asking her out on a real date. No more platonic. I want to kiss her. I want to hug her. I want her to be my forever.*

If my family ever thought I was weird back in the day… I had topped myself. But love makes us do crazy things.

Fifty-Three

Marnie

I annoyed Jen at the bookstore and Abner and Elsa at the antique store a few times a week with my missing-Eldon-to-no-end rants. But I did get through it. I got through the summer and then I faced the fact that Eldon wouldn't make it to my December book signing. I held onto the hope that I'd get some new people interested in *Arrowswan*.

If I couldn't have my happily ever after with my Elf king, I would find it on my own. I would be weird and awesome and eccentric and enjoy life as it was. The little things. *All the little joys like bagels at midnight, coffee at noon, the sound of waves crashing and rolling in the distance while I dance like a drunk fairy to "Blue". I'm fine here. I'll be okay on my own. I got this.*

Fifty-Four

Eldon

Thursday, September 26th, 2013. 3:23 PM. New York City, NY

I practiced dancing so much that I imagined my attempts as a montage in a movie. My roommates started encouraging me to work out with them and I learned better coordination. Then Anton, the one who interacted with me the most, suggested I try jump rope for cardio.

And then my co-workers started asking why I bothered to keep trying new moves when I could barely balance in a regular walking and running position. (They were really rude about my lack of coordination. I don't know why I bumped into so many doors and desks and delivery people back then.)

"I'm learning to dance for Marnie," I finally said.

"Your girlfriend?"

"No. I haven't asked her out yet."

"Why not?"

"Because, Sandie," I said, "I want it to be special."

And as if on cue, all seven girls, or women I should say, who worked on my floor, surrounded me. I sat in my chair, smelling everyone's perfumes, hair sprays, and body lotions, irritated that I couldn't get a word out about my proper first date ideas to surprise Marnie with.

But then a specific something popped into my head. *Geoff's Brass Nuts And Bolts Dating Guide.* **Rule 4: Do whatever it takes to make your dream girl feel like the only one in the room...even if it makes you feel like a total idiot.**

"Okay, okay," I said, raising my hands as if I was instructing a team of overeager superheroes. "Who here knows how to work with leather? My silhouette has to scream 'warrior'. I want to be dressed up as my Elf character Jaeger Bowen when I ask Marnie out."

I'm in an office building working as an assistant editor and most people here only know about logical emails, faxes, and not much creative juicing, but I know that everyone who wears a suit or pantsuit has a secret talent. Everyone can do something impressive that doesn't match how they look. Fact. Total fact.

"But are you really going to do it?" Brooke asked me.

"Well.."

"Are you?" Sandie leaned in the closest, her long nails scraping across my desk. "Eldon, you love her, don't you? We all see you kiss the picture of her that you have framed right here. Admit it. You are obsessed with her. Beyond obsessed."

I'm so red. My face must be so red. I ran my hands through my hair as they all smiled at me, proud of themselves that they knew how I really felt.

"Yes," I said.

Brooke pointed at a few in the group. "Three of us are pros at cosplay. All aspects of it. They can help."

"I'd show you what my character looks like," I said, "but I'm horrible at drawing."

"Then just tell me." Sandie pulled up a chair and sat beside me, squishing us both in my desk space. "I'll draw him."

Seeing how serious she was and that she was ready with a sketch pad and colored pencils that someone had tossed to her, I agreed.

I explained everything in detail about how I imagined Jaeger Bowen to be in his full warrior superhero glory, and within twenty minutes Sandie had a complete color sketch of him in the costume that I wanted to wear.

"Wow." I studied the immaculate art of my character, in love with it. "Yeah. That's it. I think Marnie will love this."

"I think she'll faint," Shelley said as she carried a box of donut holes across the office.

"No, she'll shriek and jump up and down," someone else said.

I smiled at the enthusiasm they all had for my plan.

"But only if you actually follow through and ask her out on that date. A real date." Sandie poked me in the chest with a pen. "No wimping out, Eldon."

"I won't."

I didn't really believe that my co-workers would actually make the costume for me. But they did. I ended up going over to Sandie's studio apartment a few times leading up to December in order for her to take measurements and perfect the whole vibe of the costume. Of course, dressed up as Jaeger Bowen, it was more than a costume to me. I felt like I was home. It WAS me.

* * *

Monday, October 28th, 2013. 4:45 PM.

I kept feeling like I was in a make-up trailer on the set of a massive budget fantasy movie. Except that the music that they played in the studio apartment was too vulgar for my liking.

"How's it looking, Elf king?" Brooke asked as she faced the mirror with me.

"Amazing," I said softly. "This is exactly how I pictured Jaeger would look in his complete, epic form." I tilted my head, grinning as I took in the spectacular and quality outfit.

The dark blue cloak that brushed the floor, the warrior boots, the silver and black layers that formed my tunic and leggings combo, the grey leather gauntlets and red leather pauldrons… *All of this epic beyond words. Just leaving me shaking with excitement at how I look. Marnie is gonna freak out.* I also wore the male version of a silver diadem or circlet on my head which I called an "elvish regalia emblem". Never wore anything like it before and the girls custom made that for me.

"Thank you," I said. "You don't even know how much this means."

"Well," Sandie said with a laugh as she carried a box of pizza to the center of the room, "just go get your girl, Jaeger Bowen. No payment required."

Get her I will, I told myself. "Now I need to schedule the flight home."

Fifty-Five

Eldon

Saturday, December 7th, 2013. 10:05 AM. New York City, NY

I was at the airport. I had my luggage. And I was in Elf mode.

Not only did I quit my job without telling friends and family, but I was talked into walking out of the city office building in an epic march where my co-workers lined the hallways and cheered for me as I went out the doors. All of that commotion happening among sweeping warrioresque tunes from *The Return Of The King* soundtrack.

AND I got a wedding invite from Geoff in November. He was apparently getting married in March and wanted me to be there to celebrate that…which was weird to me since he and I had butted heads on a lot. But I did say I was coming and I checkedmarked on the invitation that I was bringing a date.

Dressed up fully for the first time as my elvish superhero character Jaeger Bowen, I knew I would get nothing but stares as I boarded the plane bound for home. But this time I didn't feel awkward.

A guy across the aisle asked an obvious question: "Where are you going? You one of those actors for kid parties?"

"Nope," I said. "I'm going to ask my dream girl out."

The guy continued to give me a weird look. But the lady next to me held up her hand in what I could only assume was a high-five.

Some people get it, I thought. *Some see the magic.*

I had a few flights to get through to reach California, and on each one, each time I went to my seat, I found myself more and more at ease with what I wanted and who I was.

One long thought went over and over in my head as I browsed a bookstore in one of the airport terminals: *I'm going home to my girl, and I really wish I had some epic orchestral music playing while I walk toward her in slow motion as Jaeger Bowen.*

* * *

2:40 PM. San Luis Obispo, CA

Right when the final flight landed I got out my phone and called Mark. I knew he was still local. He wasn't the type of person to readily ditch his hometown.

"Eldon?" he said, sounding totally confused.

"Yeah, it's me. I need a favor."

"Been awhile since I heard from you, man. What do you need? You still in New York?"

I thought a moment, silently holding the phone to my ear as I looked at the doors that led outside. Then I said, "Can you pick me up from the airport?"

"Well, yeah I guess. Wait. So, you're back? Why?"

"Just come pick me up. I need you to drive me to the bookstore."

"Which one?"

"You know the one, man. Where Marnie and I would write in all the time."

"Ohhhh, really?" he asked.

I heard a smile in his voice and abruptly ended the call, knowing he would be on his way whether I kept dishing details or not.

* * *

3:37 PM

Mark had nothing but pure glee on his face the second he pulled up to the curb in his sporty green sedan. He shook his head and laughed as I wordlessly threw my luggage in the back and sat in the passenger seat.

"Should I ask questions now or later, El?"

"It's very simple," I said as we veered back onto the road. "I think Marnie is the—"

"The what? The one? Yeah sure. Remember that girl with the typewriter and wand collection I went out with twice? I felt something strong but she wasn't it. Definitely not. Not after that humiliating night…"

"It's instinct, Mark," I said. "And God's timing."

"Guys don't have instinct." Mark glanced in the rear view mirror and made a sudden lane change. "I mean, we sort of do, but it's in a southernly direction."

I grimaced at what he was referring to. "Please, don't. You sound like Geoff."

"Oh hey, you know he's getting married?"

"Yeah. Got the invite a few weeks ago."

"You're not asking Marnie out just to have a date for his wedding are you?"

"No. I'm not a jerk. I love her."

Mark looked at me as he briefly tapped his horn. "Really? How do you know she hasn't been caught up in another guy's arms?"

"I don't. But I'm making my stand now."

"Better late than never."

"I had to think about it," I said. "Plus, you know, the whole forced to work in a city company because my parents paid for college."

"Yeah," Mark agreed. "That sucks. Your mom is gonna be pissed."

"I don't care. Marnie is my future."

"Wow. Listen to you, man. Stubborn balls."

I rolled my eyes, hitting my head on the back of the seat. "Shut up, Mark."

"Sorry." He chuckled at my disdain for his dirty verbiage. "So, where did you buy that costume?"

"They made it for me."

"Who did?"

"The girls who wouldn't stop flirting with me at the office. They made me confess my love for Marnie. I had to. Otherwise they would've thought I was shy and pretending not to like them."

Mark grinned as he took a piece of gum out of his glove compartment and said, "What'd you do? Stand on a brick wall and yell about how you're obsessed with Marnie's eyes and hair? How you can't stand not being able to kiss her in the rain? How you wish you could lay in bed with her at two in the morning eating peanut butter cereal?"

"Dude," I said, giving him a please-stop-because-I'm-getting-a-headache look. "What are you talking about?"

Mark's amused smile turned into a semi-creepy cackle. "Ha. Gotcha."

Psh. Yeah. Way to make me feel like an extra sappy syrupy sap, man. I felt so cool like two hours ago.

* * *

But as I got out of Mark's car and approached the bookstore, thinking of how surprised Marnie would be to see me, I knew that I had to keep my even bigger surprise a secret for a little longer. No one, not friends or family or former co-workers, knew what I had planned for February. The culmination of all my desires and ideas I'd had since meeting Marnie.

Fifty-Six

Marnie

4:40 PM

I was honestly disappointed with my sales that day. I knew I wasn't a big famous author, but I kept hoping that I'd at least be able to sell and sign five copies before closing. I wandered from my author table in the front of store, to the center section where I chatted with Jen and drank more black coffee. I was wearing a dark cloak, light blue floor-length dress, amethyst tiara, and exceedingly sparking white boots along with my pointy ears. I felt fabulous.

"Marnie, would you mind bringing me that yellow box?"

"The one by the register?" I called to Jen.

"Yes."

I went to pick it up off the counter, wondering for a moment if I should set my coffee cup down or not, when a voice stopped me. A very familiar voice.

"Miss Koehn, would you sign a copy of your book for me?"

I whirled around. In the span of three seconds I shrieked, dropped my coffee, and had both hands pressed to my mouth.

No way. He didn't. Omg.

I backed up as Eldon stepped toward me. A grin slowly took over his face as he saw my shock. "Hi, Marnie."

This, I thought. *Wildest. Dream. Come. True.*

"Eldon…" I breathed.

"Marnie," he said again. "Hi."

"Hi." I glanced down at the coffee I had spilled and then looked over my shoulder. Just to be sure I wasn't going crazy and to make myself laugh instead of cry, I asked in a loud voice, "Jen, are you seeing what I'm seeing?"

Jen laughed as she helped a customer search for a book. "Yes. Eldon's here, Marnie. Right here in my store."

I smiled, starting to reach out to him, and then shying away. "Why?" I asked. "You came for a visit?"

His shoulders lifted as he sighed deep. "I quit my job."

"You what?"

"It's not that important. Mark said I could stay with him at his place."

Oh Eldon, I thought. *You really came back. You're really here.* "Did you come here straight from the airport?"

"I did. And I have a very important question to ask you, Marnie."

"Yeah?"

"Do you want to go on a date with me?"

A date. Eldon asked me. My Elf king asked me if I want to go out with him. A real date. "Really?"

"Really."

"Is this the official date?"

"It is. After your book signing of course. I can help you attract discerning book buyers with my amazing costume."

I giggled at his flamboyant twirl. "Is this your Jaeger Bowen look?"

"Yeah. Every inch of me." He half-smiled. "And I'd say we match."

Looking down at my own elvish outfit, I could feel myself getting dizzy. My pulse was unbelievably fast.

From a corner in the back of the store, Jen called out, "You guys look like you're ready for a fantasy photo shoot. You should do that outside."

"We totally should," Eldon said. He winked at me as we went over to my table.

But I didn't care about books or photo shoots or coffee in that moment. I wanted to go on our date. I wanted to experience the magic of being epic Elves together in public.

Fifty-Seven

Eldon

6:20 PM

I was not successful in getting more buyers for Marnie's book, but she didn't seem to care. She just kept staring at me as I sat next to her. The pure joy and passion in her brown eyes stole my heart again and again. And her mouth. I looked at the softness of her mouth. Her lips.

Dinner alone with her was nothing short of amazing. She let me choose the restaurant and I picked one with an award-winning ocean view. I filled her in on all the crazy people I had met in New York City, smiling at the way she giggled like a little fairy and toyed with her curls. We were still in our Elf garb and got plenty of looks from people, but neither of us were bothered.

It was during our walk along the pier that things shot up a level. Marnie had bought herself some glow-in-the-dark jellyfish earrings from a touristy shop and was struggling to put them in, when all at once, both earrings slipped from her hands and flew over the edge of the pier. Marnie looked down at the dark water and said dryly, "Well, at least they get to be free now."

I chuckled at her dorkiness. She said the jellyfish earrings were free… as if they were live animals. It made no sense.

Marnie laughed at herself, leaning on the railing for balance as she realized how ridiculous she sounded.

Her laugh, I thought. *Her musical, happy laugh. The sparkle in her eyes. How perfect she looks in her dress. And she's barefoot like a wild woman on the germy pier. I love how she defies logic.*

"I love you, Marnie," I said.

She met my eyes, blushing, biting her lip like she wanted to kiss me. Like she wanted to say something back. I let her lean into me and grabbed her hair, twisting my fingers in her curls. "I love you," I said again.

A timid smile remained on her face. She wouldn't stop biting her lip. I wanted to keep saying it… I wanted her to know how madly in love I had fallen. But before I could say the three sweet words again, she kissed me. She swung her arms around my neck and pressed her chest against mine, sucking all the air from my lungs.

"I love you too, El," she whispered when she pulled away.

"C'mere," I said, bringing her back. I gripped her waist, nuzzling my face into her neck. "You don't know how long I've wanted to do this, Marnie. How long I've wanted to kiss you. Hold you."

Marnie breathed shallow as she ran her hands through my hair, digging her nails into my neck. She didn't say anything else. Just breathed.

"You're so beautiful," I said. "So full of love and life and fire."

"Elf king," Marnie said to me, sighing when I ran my lips along her cheek and ear. "My sexy Elf king."

Vow Of The Silent Kindred, I thought. *VOTSK.*

I didn't like that we would sleep in separate apartments that night, but I looked forward to what was yet to come. I wanted nothing more to honor and cherish the girl, no, the woman, who I loved. I wanted her to trust me and me to trust her. No matter how tough it got.

Vow Of The Silent Kindred

Fifty-Eight

Eldon

Sunday, December 8th, 2013. 9:45 PM. Atascadero, CA

The day after I took Marnie out and we officially became a couple… it was rather random. I needed to get my van back because I had left it at my parents' house, but I didn't want them to see me pick it up because I was afraid to have the confrontation with my mom over me quitting the city job. So I got Mark involved… and he came up with quite the scheme.

"So, what did he say I'm supposed to do again?"

"Keep watch for my parents while I start the van."

Marnie followed, ducking near the back door with me. "But why are we dressed like Neo and Trinity?"

"Mark's idea, love. Not mine."

"When are you gonna tell your mom that you quit?"

"Like a month. Are you going to stand guard with him now?"

"Sure. You're such a goofball, El. I love it." She gave me a quick kiss on the cheek and headed toward Mark who waited at the front of the house.

I knew I was crazy, but Marnie brought it out in a way I couldn't have predicted. The rush was incredible. She was my sexy, dorky spitfire.

Unfortunately, the keys were hidden in one of my mom's rainbow colored flower pots, and I had to dig through each one until I found them. I could hear Marnie giggling at something Mark was saying and almost yelled at them to shush, but I was too focused. I needed the keys. I needed to drive away with my dignity.

"Oh my fudge," I said when I felt metal in the dirt. It was the eighth flower pot I'd tried. "Yes."

Running, while staying low to the ground, my long Neo coat sweeping around my boots, I made it to my van and coughed hard in the freezing air.

"Sunglasses at night," Mark said as he came over with Marnie right behind. "I know. Bad idea." He pushed the extremely dark sunglasses up his nose. "But someone had to be Agent Smith."

"Totally," Marnie said. She was bouncy and giddy.

"I'll see you back at the apartment. Or you wanna have a late night celebratory drink?" Mark asked us.

"Oooh, let's get pancakes instead!"

We both looked at Marnie like she had gone crazy. "Pancakes at night?"

"Why not? You're wearing sunglasses at night."

"Costume, girl, costume," Mark said, motioning to himself.

"Pancakes, El!" Marnie said again to me. "Let's totally get some."

I traded winks with Mark. "See? I told you she was quirky."

"Yeah. No kidding, man."

Opening the doors to my van, I started to get in, but then I saw the lights go on in my parents' house. That never happened at this hour.

"Shoot! We gotta go! Get in your car, Mark, and drive."

But Mark sauntered up to my window with a bold smile. "Oh, Mr. Anderson," he said in an exaggerated low, slowly drawn out voice, "you disappoint me."

"Mark, I'm serious. If you don't wanna explain all my shortcomings to my parents, get your butt in your car and go."

"All right, all right." He pointed at Marnie. "Your boyfriend's a wet blanket, isn't he, doll?"

Marnie giggled. "No, he's epic."

"Psh. Saps," Mark said and ran to his car.

But I heard the smile in his voice. I knew he secretly loved me and Marnie's eccentric, adorable connection.

Fifty-Nine

Marnie

Being Eldon's girlfriend felt like a miracle. Every day that we hung out and got to trade gentle, playful affection was beautiful. Of course he was my best friend. But my best friend who was the most attractive guy ever turned into my boyfriend. I couldn't believe it was really true for weeks.

We did go through the whole Eldon meeting my parents and sister Bristol thing. Wasn't as eventful as when I first met his family. Not much to report on that day or that Christmas season. To honor each other and our values, we kept to our own residences, myself still sharing an apartment with Bristol, and Eldon sleeping on the couch at Mark's one bedroom place.

Eldon did find a job at a grocery store, working especially hard on the weekends, and he started writing more stories outside of his Jaeger Bowen adventures. The book to movie dream was something we both shared. And we never stopped trying to achieve our big writer goals.

Sixty

Eldon

⸎

Wednesday, January 15th, 2014. 2:31 PM. Arroyo Grande, CA

Marnie wore a lot of red that day. She looked like a spitfire. Like a reflection of her inner spirit. *Red lipstick. So much red. It's so sexy. So gorgeous. And the high heels and leather jacket. Whew, my baby. My darling queen.*

We exited the movie theater after seeing some epic action flick, and while holding her hand, I pointed with the other. "Marnie, you see that car over there?"

"Which one?" she asked.

I counted to five in my head and suddenly a black Lamborghini pulled up to the curb. The driver stepped out, grinning at us.

"This is Avery," I said. "Friend of a friend of Geoff. He said we could sit in his ride for a few minutes."

"For real?"

I nodded, excited and proud of myself that another surprise of mine had worked out. "For real. Go on, my love."

"Oh my gosh," Marnie said as she got into the shimmering car. "El, how did you get this lucky?"

"Oh, it's you," I said, sliding in next to her. I closed the door and took her hands in mine. "You're my luck, muffin. You always have been."

"Goofy Elf king," she giggled, leaning in to kiss me.

"My dorky Elf queen," I said. "You drive me wild."

And so... we made out. Yep. We made out for about thirty-five minutes in the back of a Lamborghini. I really owed that one to Geoff.

Sixty-One

Eldon

Friday, February 7th, 2014. 8:30 PM. San Simeon, CA

"Geoff, Mark, you guys out here?"

"Yeah, El. Waiting for the signal."

I turned off my phone when I saw Marnie come jogging back from one of the public bathrooms. I was trembling and clumsy and unable to talk to her without stumbling through my words again. To distract myself, I carried a cup of tepid coffee that I had left sitting in my van's front cup holder.

This is the night. I'm doing this. We're made to be together. Is it too soon? No. It's fine. We are cool. I don't wanna lose her. The best friend time before? The non-dating time? That counts toward this step, doesn't it?

"Hey, muffin, do you feel like taking a walk before dinner? Mark was telling me about this weird group of stars and they look really cool from here. I think he said it's like a new constellation or something."

"Really?" Marnie glanced up and then back at me. She sifted through her purse as we walked toward the pier.

"You know what," I said, "I gotta take a picture of this."

"Of what? It's pitch black."

"You see that cluster of stars up there?" I pointed up from behind her shoulder, feeling chills when my arm brushed against her soft skin. *Ugh. The off-the-shoulder shirt. Marnie girl!* "They are extra bright. See them? I can use that scene for inspiration when writing the next Jaeger Bowen story."

Sixty-Two

Marnie

8:21 PM

I saw Eldon bend to set his coffee cup on the ground, wondering why he couldn't just hold his phone with one hand to take a picture. But I looked up at the night sky, trying to see the stars he was talking about. All I saw was the moon hidden behind a light veil of fog. Definitely not worth the effort for a phone camera's snapshot.

"El, I don't see the group of stars you're talking about. Where were you looking?"

Then I looked back at him, nearly dropping my own phone. He was down on one knee.

"Marnie Staysha Koehn, will you marry me?"

The Earth stopped. I felt every tingle, every emotion, every ounce of love colliding and rising into my chest and through my veins with an icy hot vigor. Like a beautiful shock. A beautiful chain reaction of lightning and sea. Jaeger Bowen, Elf Hero of The Aetlanir Sea was going to be Arrowswan, Queen of Ranefire's husband.

Just us. It's just us on this pier.

But the first thing to come out of my mouth was: "But I don't have my ears on."

And we both laughed.

"I want to marry you with or without the Elf ears, baby. I want you to be my love forever."

I nodded, irritated at feeling tears sting my eyes. "You know I do too, Eldon."

"So, a yes?"

"Yes. Yes a thousand times," I said.

He smiled, and after a prolonged moment of me nodding vigorously and jumping up and down, he put the ring on my finger, standing up to embrace me. "You sure it's not too soon?"

"No. It's just right." I let out an overjoyed shriek after he kissed my lips and I laid my face against his hair. "What if I said I wanted to get married in December?"

"This December, right?" he asked, clearly wanting to get the show on the road.

"Yes. Can you wait until then for that… special night?" *Although it can take the entire honeymoon to build to that big moment and I'd still be excited.*

"You are more than worth the wait, baby. Just promise you keep the sweet kisses and cuddles coming."

"You got it," I said, sealing the promise with a long, passionate kiss in which Eldon dipped me and expertly spun me around like we were ballroom dancers.

Then came music. Loud music. Out of nowhere. I whipped my head to look for the source. "Hey. I know that song! That's—"

"'Blue,'" Eldon finished for me.

"But where?"

"Don't you feel like dancing, Marn?"

"Dancing? You dance now?"

Eldon winked and said, "Watch me."

My jaw dropped when he started moving with the music. Like REALLY moving. I was so turned on I can't even tell you. And he had this smile… this heart-stopping smile.

"C'mon, baby. Isn't this your favorite song?"

I jumped in, moving in sync with him, both of us expertly shuffling to the beat.

"El, how are you doing this?"

"You like it? I taught myself. Starting working out and everything."

We talked as we spun around each other. "Wow. You work out now too?"

"Jump rope for cardio."

"Hot," I said. "Very hot. I love when men jump rope."

We went faster to keep up with the music, Eldon tripping a few times while still looking sexy. The song abruptly changed and we crashed into each other, laughing hysterically.

"Who is doing the music?" I asked. "Seriously?"

The music sputtered to a stop.

"Happy engagement!" four voices suddenly screamed out, and Geoff, Mark, Tawny, and some random dude ran toward us for a group hug.

Wha?? I stumbled forward when Tawny squeezed me. "Yeah, girl! Of course we wouldn't miss seeing this! And I got pictures of it!"

"You took pictures of us?" I said "Out in the dark? But I didn't see any camera flashes."

"Um, ninja photographer, girlfriend," Tawny said, waving her hand in front of my face as if she was showing off some unseen magical powers.

Eldon was yanked away by the guys and they were all hollering for him. I could hear him asking Geoff why there was a strange dude among us.

"Oh," Geoff said, "this is my brother Cooper. He's been hanging around while I ramp up wedding details with my woman."

I turned around to congratulate Geoff on his upcoming wedding, but was bombarded by his just-introduced-to-us brother.

"Marnie, you are so fire!" Cooper said, sounding incredibly drunk. "You and Eldon are hot together. Dayum, woman!"

I looked at Eldon for help and he came over, gently pushing Cooper out of my face. "Let's get some late dinner," he said. And then he dramatically pointed to Geoff. "Geoff's buying!"

We all laughed when Geoff pretended not to hear Eldon. "But okay," he said. "If my man El is also engaged I guess I'll take the hit."

* * *

10:30 PM

The restaurant we picked was more traditional Italian than seafood, and it was a blast sitting squished together in a big booth. I kept looking at my ring, squealing with Tawny as she began spewing wedding venue ideas even though it wasn't hers to plan…

"So, Tawny," Eldon said as he reached for the bread, "how'd the pictures turn out?"

The table fell quiet. Everyone looked at Tawny with her blue hair and long, pastel nails that she drummed repetitively while she talked.

"Here," she said, passing the camera to Eldon.

"Oh wow! A real camera? Not a phone app?"

I giggled at Eldon's surprisingly sarcastic words.

"Yep. I took at least twenty," Tawny said. She forked a piece of salad and gave a flirty smile to the other guys.

"Well…" Eldon started. He covered his mouth with one hand, hiding a smile, and then without saying anything passed the camera to me.

I clicked through the pictures. Not a single one was clear. All blurry. All of them. I didn't like calling people out on their faults and I wasn't about to out Tawny. But Eldon was coughing into his napkin in an effort to disguise his laughter.

"So?" Mark said, showing interest in the middle of devouring a giant steak. "Lemme see."

"Tawny," I said.

"Yeah?" She looked at me, smiling brightly, completely oblivious to the error.

"The pictures are blurry," I finally said. "Eldon and I look like we're on a carousel that is stuck in the super fast mode."

Instead of being sheepish or apologetic, Tawny grinned wider, picked up her glass of champagne, and raised it in the air. She looked like she was about to make an impromptu toast. But she dropped her head on the table and laughed harder than I've heard her laugh.

"I'm guessing you all had drinks before you came to help me surprise Marnie?" Eldon said.

"Oh yeah," Cooper said in a deep, goofy voice. "We sure did, man."

Eldon and I traded feel-like-a-parent-already looks, rolled our eyes at the same time with a shake of the head, and leaned in for a dramatic, out of context kiss.

Seriously, I wish that we could've had like an end credit scene start rolling right then. It was so odd and funny and we just had the weirdest friends.

But so not boring. What a night.

Sixty-Three

Eldon

Once engaged, Marnie made it her mission to find us a private dance studio and start practicing showstopping choreography for our first dance. My moves had impressed her to the point that she couldn't keep her hands off me even in public. She was not shy about affection and I was getting used to her wild side. There was still a line drawn that we didn't cross, but other than that… it got quite spicy.

"This is my cousin's studio," Marnie said when we walked into a very pink building. "And this…"

I let out a gasp when I followed her into the next room. It was all mirrors. Every direction you looked was a mirror. "Marn, I'm not sure I like the idea of seeing my mistakes so clearly."

"But you're great, baby. Now we can pick songs!"

"Oh, I know," I said, shrugging off my jacket. "Bet I can guess what song you want to do our first dance to."

Marnie threw off her cloak and kicked off her shoes. "Yeah? Well, I want an entire medley to play. Like a mixy-matchy version of all the songs we like."

"Want me to guess?"

"Okay."

I circled her as I pretended to struggle in my thinking. "Hmm. I think it's "The Time Of Your Life" by Randy Newman. From *A Bug's Life* soundtrack."

Marnie smiled but didn't respond. She came up to me, wrapping her arms around my waist. Tilted her head as I touched my nose to hers.

"What, baby?" I asked. "What's the suspense for?"

"You're just so freakin' cute, Jaeger."

"So are you, Arrowswan."

"And yeah, that's one of the songs I'll dance with you to."

"I can't wait," I said. And I kissed her long and slow. "Let's wow the crowd, my queen."

Sixty-Four

Marnie

"You know I'm not a professional by any means, baby," Eldon said.

"Neither am I. It's just fun."

We set aside an hour each day to rehearse our first dance, laughing when we tried out weird and dorky moves. I got to watch Eldon do push-ups and other workouts in front of me and us jumping rope together. It was strange to our friends that we never took off our shirts or wore super revealing clothes when working out... they figured we should just do it already because we were in love and a serious couple. But we mutually agreed to wait for the honeymoon (no matter how hard it was to wait) to show the parts of our bodies that were more... you know.

I couldn't have been more excited to be dancing with my Elf king. We were so weird next to each other always laughing and tickling each other on the floor and then wildly making out in our sweaty after-the-workout-mess against the mirrors.

So proud of my Eldon for becoming bolder and stronger and unafraid to be who he wanted to be. The dancer that he turned into... so fire. So, so fire. I LOVED it.

Sixty-Five

Eldon

Saturday, March 8th, 2014. 5:55 PM. San Luis Obispo, CA

Ah, yes. The wedding day of the friend that I never thought would settle down. Geoff. There were a few specific highlights from that whole spectacle, most of which involved Marnie and I tearing it up on the dance floor.

Sixty-Six

Marnie

Saturday, March 8th, 2014. 5:55 PM. San Luis Obispo, CA

We walked into the reception five seconds after the bride and groom, realizing our mistake when everyone gave us disgruntled stares.

"We didn't time that well, did we, muffin?" Eldon whispered.

"Nope," I said, leaning closer as he squeezed my hand. "I think we stole their thunder."

"Well, I think you look far more tantalizing in your silk dress and cloak than she does in her gown."

I looked to the left as we meandered through tables, trying to find ours. "Not now, Eldon. They've got eyes to kill."

"But we didn't do anything," he said. "We're epic."

Our name cards were at the furthest table back, among three other couples who suddenly claimed that they had to use the restroom.

"It's like the Red Sea parting," Eldon said. "Total Vow Of The Silent Kindred moment."

"They're not gonna like when we show off our moves on the dance floor, are they?" I asked.

"No, baby," he said. "More thunder will be taken."

* * *

About twenty minutes after our poorly timed entrance, Geoff and his bride came over to us. We stood up to have what I thought would be a heated conversation, and Geoff did indeed have words. "I thought you knew this wasn't a costume theme wedding, man."

"This isn't a costume," Eldon said. "Jaeger always wears this kind of thing."

I was encouraged when the bride kindly said with a smile, "It's okay. You two look cute."

"Oh, thank you, Marisse," Eldon told her while shooting a combination mocking-cocky face at Geoff.

"Babe," Geoff said to Marisse, "don't encourage it. I swear he's not dressed like a normal person since high school."

I smiled, admiring Eldon as he stood confidently in his silver cloak, black leggings, and high-collared shirt. *My man. My Elf king. All in one fantastically delicious package.*

"You look too much like a Disney prince!" Geoff whined.

"Jaeger isn't a prince," Eldon said firmly. "This is his fancy kingly attire. Isn't that right, Arrowswan?"

"Yep," I said. "And I'm wearing Arrowswan's fancy dress. Usually she is more casual."

"Okay. Just okay." Geoff held up his arms in protest. "You two just keep the showmanship to a minimum. All right?"

Eldon and I faked that we understood him and shrugged with half-smiles. I would have left the subject alone but as Geoff and Marisse started to go visit with other tables, I just had to say, "Geoff, excuse me for saying this in front of your new bride, but since when do you care about proper etiquette? The first time I came into the apartment you were just in your boxers."

Geoff's new wife looked startled at the news but then burst into laughter. "Are you serious, babe?" she said.

"I'm getting you back for mentioning that," Geoff said in a half-teasing tone to me. He pointed intensely at me and Eldon and back to himself. "Dance floor."

* * *

8:44 PM

The dance floor was crowded, loud, sweaty, and the bass was killer.

Eldon and I had some relatively chill moments just swaying together, lost in each other's eyes, kissing every time he spun me around.

But Geoff and his Marisse kept coming near, bumping us aside with their hips. Mostly was Geoff's doing I think.

"You can lead a raccoon to trash but you can't make him eat it," Eldon said in his cute, oddball time-for-a-nonsensical-backward-idiom way when he saw Geoff openly staring at my chest. It didn't help that I had taken off my cloak and displayed my shoulders and the lowest neckline I'd shown yet.

"Keep your eyes on your own woman, man," Eldon said.

Geoff grinned when I moved so that he couldn't get a view. "Hey, I promise I'm only into my wife. But your girl is amazing, El. Truth."

Much appreciated, I thought. *It's still fun when the boys battle over me.*

But at some point I also discovered I had a real rival on the dance floor. A girl with miles long legs, a dress that was as fitted as plastic wrap around a sandwich, and a face full of false eyelashes, puckery lips, and an annoyingly attractive nose ring. AND she would not stop staring at Eldon's gorgeous hair and ass.

That evil woman was apparently Cooper's (Geoff's brother) girl-friend. And I knew she had to be stopped before Eldon reacted to her ultra sexy movements.

Sixty-Seven

Eldon

9:22 PM

I had never felt so alive in a crowd. I usually hated crowds but I was hyper and giddy and pumped. Marnie pulled me into performing some extra hot dance moves, and slowly we took up the whole floor with our performance. Then something amazing, almost miraculous happened. Marnie ran toward me and I grabbed her in a strong whirl, lifting her above my head. And she stayed there. My arms held her up like I was Hercules.

"Whoa, baby," Marnie said. "Did you know you could do this?"

"I didn't."

"This is such a turn on, El, but you better put me down. They stopped the music."

What?! Jealous much?? I thought. *They don't want us showing off... not fair.*

They halted the music when I had Marnie in the air. But then the second our feet had left the designated dance floor it went back on.

Man, this crowd is hatin'.

Sixty-Eight

Marnie

9:31 PM

Starving, I looked back to the tables with food. I wasn't gonna let them take it all away and replace it with the cake yet. *I need savory carbs.*

"Hey, El." I placed a chip in my mouth as I waved him over.

He kept his eyes on the dance floor, all smiley and panting. *I have goosebumps looking at his long sweaty hair.*

"Promise you won't dance with someone else," I said.

"I won't. You know I would never do that."

"Well, Cooper's girlfriend keeps trying to call you over with her hips."

"Don't worry, muffin. You're my queen."

"But that one out there is a wily lioness."

"You have me," Eldon said. "I only see you. I only see your body, your face, your so-adorable-I-wanna-eat-you lips."

"That's good," I said and intensely sipped the rest of my wine.

"You ready to get back out there, Arrowswan?"

I grinned at the spark in his eyes. "Lift me again, Jaeger. Make 'em think they should all be sitting front row at a badass contemporary ballet."

"You're a little drunk, aren't you, babe?"

"Just fierce. Tipsy and fierce," I said as we charged back into the mass of partiers.

"Whoa, Marnie! Marnie!"

I didn't think to look at who I just ran into, and suddenly Eldon and I were sprawled in the middle of the floor… with the bride and groom on top of us. The music sputtered like a dry cough at the end of a cold and everyone froze in place. *Yup. This is embarrassing. But what isn't?*

Sixty-Nine

Eldon

Saturday, November 8th, 2014. 6:42 PM. San Luis Obispo, CA

Marnie and I, in accordance with our shared personal values and morals, didn't want any bachelor or bachelorette parties. We were firm on it. It didn't matter if the setting was neutral or PG. We just said no to it all. But, as many friends like to do… Geoff and Mark and even blurry-picture-taker Tawny, decided that they had to have the last say in the matter. And the result was… *cue combined sigh eye roll…* Quite the event.

Seventy

Marnie

6:55 PM

"Baby," Eldon whispered once we got into the restaurant, "I really think we've been set up."

To be fair: The effort to even find the place using Geoff's squirrelly directions was a pain in the butt. And there were live ducks running loose in the restaurant. And also, we were the only people there. Despite the not-so-appetizing first look of it all, I had a hunch it was going to get very, very funny. I was bracing myself the whole time for the punchline of the night.

"I'm sorry, Marnie, but who in their right mind would name a restaurant 'Soup In The Dark' and fill it with a company of ducks?"

"It's sorta cute," I said, amazed at myself that I hadn't burst out laughing yet. "I think we should play along if it is a stupid prank."

"Okay. But I'm worried."

I led the way, choosing a table in the center of the room, and sat on a chair that felt and sounded like it should have been replaced sixty years ago.

"Did Geoff ever mention that his second cousin had a restaurant?" I asked.

"Nope." Eldon sat across from me, looking around with a slight scowl that I wasn't used to seeing. It was sweet that he wanted the best for me and not some one star service. "Don't delve too deep in it, love. I think all of this is a huge, huge disaster waiting to blow up."

And just as he said the words "blow up" there was a real explosion in the kitchen. He grabbed my arm, pulling me under the table with him. "See?!" he said. "They're trying to severely injure us!"

Okay, I thought. *He has to be faking this paranoia.* "Why are you all frantic?"

"I do not want my friends to humiliate you, baby. In any way. You have been through enough in this harsh world."

"It's fine," I said. "They're not out to get us, Eldon. And why are we still under the table?"

"Explosion." He kissed my ear and whispered, "Let's just get up slowly."

We did get up. Plopped back into our chairs. And then we saw Tawny appear out of the kitchen, or someone who looked like her, dressed up as a pirate queen. She was fake playing a fiddle, but music still emitted from it.

Umm....what? We looked at each other and I saw Eldon trying hard not to smile.

"All right! What the hedge happened to the place? I was gone for ten minutes!" Mark came charging through the front door, wearing super flashy rockstar-ish clothes and a blond long haired wig.

Oh no.

Then he jumped into some dorky monologue and poem centered around ducks while Tawny clumsily tossed drinks and chips at our table.

It was so dark in there. Only the floor was dimly lit. Then the lights completely went out and thunderous music started. One of the songs we both loved: "My Sharona". When the lights popped back on… there was Mark, Geoff, and Tawny on a makeshift stage pretending to play and sing the old school song. We heard screams and cheers and almost fell over when a hundred people rushed through the doors and into the restaurant with us, everyone sprinting to find a chair at a table as if they were being timed to get there. Several other songs magically came on from various old school eighties movies.

A flash mob ensued.

And then it rained yellow rubber ducks inside the restaurant. Which finally had Eldon laughing hysterically.

Seventy-One

Eldon

Saturday, December 13th, 2014. 4 PM. Pinecrest, CA

Our wedding day. I was anxious to see Marnie in her dress, but doubly anxious to read my vows. I think we both had tunnel vision that entire day. We did greet our families and friends and made certain that the groomsmen and bridesmaids were all in a relatively happy vibe. Fun fact: Marnie's bridesmaids were all dressed in baby blue dresses, dark cloaks, and pointy ears. My groomsmen were wearing the typical black tie stuff despite the cold. Yes, we were outside surrounded by forest and snow. The dream.

"Can I ask why you are wearing white too? I thought that was just for the bride."

I sighed at Geoff's comment and how he kept poking my shoulder.

"It's an honor thing for us," I said. "Honor plus divulging in our fantasy worlds. This is how we imagine Jaeger Bowen and Arrowswan to look if they got married."

"Logical. For you that's very logical."

"It is." I kept facing forward, willing myself not to throw a punch to make him stop talking.

"All right, El. Won't argue."

"Good."

"But your cloak is sparkly. That's not really cool."

Oh, for the love of goblins. Can't he shut up for a minute? We have an entire ceremony to get through and now I feel stupid for even letting him stand up here with me. "Why can't I be sparkly?" I said, turning around to give Geoff a prideful look. "I'm an Elf king."

"Then where are the ears?"

"Marnie and I agreed not to wear our ears today."

"Wow."

"Yep. Authentic selves."

"Yeah," Geoff said shortly. "Minus the Elf attire."

Oh for goodness sake, I thought. *Stoooop talking, man.*

"Shut up, Geoff," Mark said.

I smiled as I faced the aisle again. *Thanks, Mark. You've earned a position in my future fantasy army.*

Seventy-Two

Marnie

4:25 PM

A winter wedding. I was in love with how the decorations turned out and excited beyond excited for the dancing, catered food, the variety of desserts, and the custom designed coffee bar for those who wanted iced and hot coffee with their evening cinnamon rolls and red velvet cupcakes.

This. This right here.

That magical second when you lock eyes from the end of the aisle. I only have one word to describe what I felt when I looked back at Eldon. Adoration. For a minute I was nervous remembering that I didn't have my ears on. *But I'm walking down the aisle to the ethereal sound of Aragorn and Arwen's theme. It's perfection.*

How do brides not run down the aisle? I kept thinking, *this can't be a mirage. This can't be a mirage. Please be real when I get to you. Please please don't disappear when I reach out my hand to yours... my Eldon Fergus Cornade. My Jaeger Bowen.*

But I touched his hands, held onto him as he looked me up and down with tears in his beautiful blue eyes. "It's like we're in a movie. You're everything, Marnie," he whispered.

I couldn't speak without getting choked up so I just smiled.

"My wonder-eyed spitfire," Eldon said to me, his voice cracking as he quickly wiped tears from his face. "You're scintillating, Arrowswan."

Seventy-Three

Eldon

5:01 PM

When we got to the vows, I had to work past a few shaky breaths and the constant threat of tears. Seeing Marnie… how perfect, angelic, the most beautiful woman in the world. She healed and broke my heart all at once. Powerful Elf queen. Her piercing yet gentle gaze.

"I dreamed of meeting and falling in love with a princess, but I couldn't have imagined such a wonderful, adorable, and perfectly quirky woman. You are everything and more, my love. You are my constellation in the night and my blue sky in the morning. You are my song, dance, joy, and passion. I will keep you safe and love you until the day the Lord calls me Home. And I pray that His hand will be on our lives and our dreams as we grow higher together."

Looking up from my paper, I saw Marnie grinning and blushing. I went on.

"Every morning births from the darkness before it. And I want us to always remember that there is a morning. There is sun. There is light and love even in the roughest of nights. I will do everything I can to show you why I chose and will choose you every day to be my wife."

Looking at Marnie again, I saw her biting her lip. She was dying to kiss me.

"Sometimes," I said, clearing my throat when I felt tears welling up, "the only way forward is to make a fool of yourself. And you, my beautiful, have helped me unlock all the awesome crazy parts of me that I was afraid to show. I always had faith in God, but now I trust His timing and plan more than ever." I lowered the paper, feeling a mix of hot and cold chills trickle down my spine. "I love you, Marnie. So much."

Seventy-Four

Marnie

5:20 PM

In the minute of silence following Eldon's incredibly poetic speech, I could hear the sniffles and sighs among our guests. "I don't think I can top that," I said, looking down at the little paper I held in my hands.

Chuckles swept through everyone like a breeze, giving me a joyful push to go on with my turn.

"Eldon, you are more than I prayed for." I met his eyes as he cocked his head, sniffing back more tears. *So sweet. He's so sensitive.* "You're the most loving, gentle, kind-hearted person I know. You're adorable, sexy, and crazy romantic. I know I can count on you as we continue forward together. I will support you through the good and ugly days, and I promise I won't put eight hundred rubber ducks in your van again."

More laughter around us. Eldon chuckled too.

"But, I don't think I've seen anyone laugh as hard as you did on that day. And your laugh is the cutest, happiest sound. You make me so happy and you give so much love. This life isn't about what we do but about who we are. And I'll never stop loving who you are, Eldon. I'll never give you up. I want to be yours forever. Til death do us part."

I'm ready for my kiss now. I'm ready to be your wife.

We did reach the kiss, and once it was done, and I looked at both our rings, and back up at Eldon's eyes, I felt a peace and contentment that nothing could compare to. He made me feel safe, loved, and one hundred percent accepted as myself.

Seventy-Five

Eldon

7:40 PM

My mind, my body was solely focused on Marnie. The whole night. Our first dance was fantastic. Memorable and hard to beat in my opinion.

"Ready?" I whispered to her as we stood back to back on the dance floor.

"Yes," she whispered back.

Barefoot on the smooth wood. Both our breathing fast and intense. *Slow it down. Breathe slow. We got this.*

We performed our fantasy ballroom-inspired choreographed dance to an epic medley of all our favorite movie soundtracks. And then it switched to a mashup of 80s rock and 90s techno for everyone else to jump in and dance to with us.

Oh, and here is an eccentric fun fact: We specifically played the last minute of "A Bug's Life Suite" as our recessional song. The dramatic crescendo with the orchestral score when we kissed to everyone's cheers was pure magic.

Seventy-Six

Marnie

11:31 PM

And then it was the first honeymoon night. The first time we shared a hotel room and a bed. And I pretty much lost my mind the second I watched Eldon take off his shirt. He folded it and placed it on a chair before picking up the remote and turning on the TV.

"Hey, Eldon," I said with a gesture to the bathroom, "I'm gonna brush my teeth."

"Can't you do it after?"

"After?"

"Yeah. After." He grinned and laid the remote to the side. "I'm nervous too, baby, but I think I'm less nervous than you are about this whole thing. Just lay next to me. We can find a movie if that helps you relax."

I had told myself over and over that I was ready for this night. But nothing and no one could have said anything that would've prepared me for the butterflies, anxiety, and intense heat that tore through me like a fire and hurricane melded into one. *I love this man with everything, but how am I gonna get past this awkward, roller coaster-drop nervousness moment?*

I grabbed his wrist as he leaned in, sitting up and pushing against his chest. "Wait."

"What's wrong?"

"What if I'm not good enough? I'm not like those girls who always flirted with you. I probably don't have their same, I don't know, fire and talent."

Eldon chuckled, running his fingers through my curls. "You forget, love, that I'm in the same boat. I only know what I know because I love you and we just had our dream wedding. I'm scared too."

In the midst of kissing in the dark, our bodies as close as they could be, the silence was shattered by the loudest, most symphonic fart. Mine. I thought I would be embarrassed by that happening, and I was. But the second I let that sound loose (I swear like a foghorn), Eldon had fallen back on the bed laughing and I fell on top of him laughing even harder.

That was our first night of being husband and wife. We couldn't get another kiss or hot maneuver in because of the constant thought of my fart. Not totally proud honestly, but it made for one memorable wedding night.

And we did make up for it. Didn't leave our room until three o'clock the next day.

* * *

Waking up next to Eldon became my new favorite thing. On the third morning of our honeymoon, he rolled over with a small smile, kissed me on the lips, and whispered a sweet, "I love you so much, baby."

"Can we just stay in bed, El? Not go down to breakfast?"

"I thought that you needed coffee to talk in the morning. It's not even seven yet."

"You're better than coffee," I said, tracing my fingertips up his chest and neck. "Wake me up, Jaeger. Give me a jump start."

"Oh, a jump start, huh?" He grinned wide and threw the covers over both of us, initiating a tickle fight that I was guaranteed to lose.

Crazy adorable. This man is so adorable I can't stand it. I love him so much it hurts.

* * *

The fifth day of our honeymoon went as follows:

"Feel like jumping rope, Marn? Gonna get a workout in."

"Not a euphemism?" I said.

Eldon laughed while taking a brand new jump rope out of his suitcase. "That would be pretty sad if that was a euphemism."

I laughed with him and agreed to join in. Didn't want my Elf king to have to work out and be all sexy alone.

We did it beside each other. Jumping rope with strong balance and coordination. It was so fun. So bonding. Euphoric.

The way his sweaty strands of hair come loose from his ponytail and stick against his face. His shirtless glory. Abs I didn't realize he had developed.

Seventy-Seven

Eldon

Wednesday, January 14th, 2015. 12:31 AM. San Luis Obispo, CA

We functioned pretty well as newlyweds. The best part to me outside of the obvious sexy time stuff was all the funny and odd habits that we both had and only learned about once moving in together. I was able to score a one bedroom apartment for us, and I slowly got back into the swing of writing screenplays. That was still where I wanted my career to go… and I wasn't giving up on partnering with Mark to make an epic movie.

I tended to write my best at night, and I had to use the bedroom as my office when Marnie wanted to watch her movies and go on her video game binges in the front living space. Sometimes Marnie worked on her books too, but once we were married, her interests and energy seemed to shift.

The most adorable thing occurred one night when I thought Marnie had already fallen asleep on the couch. I could smell something cooking. Toasting. *But it's after midnight...*

I scooted my chair forward and peered around the doorway of our bedroom to see Marnie in the kitchen. "Marnie, what are you doing?"

"It's a bagel," she said, raising it with tongs.

"A bagel at midnight?" I asked.

"Yeah. I always do this."

I watched her start putting cream cheese on it, fascinated by the choice of late night activity, and went back to work without another word.

Eight days later a t-shirt came in the mail and I handed it to Marnie while opening a fresh box of peanut butter cereal.

Marnie peed herself laughing when she saw what the t-shirt said. It read: "**Bagels At Midnight**" and had dancing cartoon bagels beneath the words.

"Your midnight routine is so darn random and adorable, baby," I said. "I couldn't resist."

Honestly. What a cutie.

Seventy-Eight

Marnie

Thursday, June 23rd, 2016. 1:15 PM. San Luis Obispo, CA

The first time we tried writing a book together didn't go as planned. We mutually agreed to work on a story that combined Arrowswan and Jaeger Bowen's adventures. The problem?

"I know Arrowswan protects all the critters and dragons," Eldon said, "and I appreciate the epic fight scenes that happen in the sky against the dark overlord… but I just can't get past the talking animals."

"Why?"

"If they read each other's minds that would work. But they shouldn't physically be talking. And Arrowswan shouldn't be able to talk to them either."

I groaned as I watched Eldon neatly shuffle his papers. "But I thought you thought it was cute."

"I don't like when animals are talking in any fashion other than the way God made them to sound. They can't sound like people. It gives me the creeps when they do."

"But you like *A Bug's Life*."

"I love it, but that's animation, and *Arrowswan* wouldn't be an animated story. Her world is real life in my mind. No cartoon moments."

I stood up, pacing when I thought of how to convince Eldon to come to my side. "But that's too serious, babe. Where's the compromise?"

Collaborating was not going to be an option. I felt it. Even though I didn't like the fact. And Eldon looked just about fed up with the debate.

"El, are you frustrated?"

"Yes," he said from behind his notebook. He took a sip of orange juice.

"Do you wanna talk about it or do you wanna work it out in the bedroom?"

He looked at me, slowly taking off his reading glasses. "Do YOU want to talk about it?"

I shook my head with a naughty grin and Eldon, without further discussion, stood, took my hand, and ran us into the bedroom.

Game over. But really, how is this losing?

Seventy-Nine

Eldon

We had a good several months of radio silence, marital bliss, and just enjoying each other in our daily and nightly routines. Things changed in a big way again in January of twenty nineteen.

Marnie walked into our bedroom barefoot wearing a thin, white crop top and tight black jeans. Whatever I was thinking immediately exited my brain.

"What's the occasion?" I asked.

"I just want to make sure you get your fun use out of me while I'm still looking and feeling sexy," she said.

"You'll always be sexy. C'mere." I started kissing down her chest as she was lying beneath me, and I heard her take a big breath.

"Eldon?"

"What?"

"We're having a baby."

"What?" I sat her up, grasping her trembling hands in mine. "Really?"

She nodded and I noticed her tears. "This is the best thing. What's wrong, babe?"

"What if I can't do it? What if I can't raise a kid in this world? Everything is so dangerous and you can't trust anyone and we have to protect them and the schools and criticisms and—"

"Marnie. Marnie…" I kissed her nose and wrapped my arms around her. "We're going to be fine. You'll do so good. I know you will."

"The whole idea of it though. It's still scary."

"I know. It's okay. I'm right with you." I held her, feeling the tension in her body. She feared raising our baby in the cold world. The hardness of society. I understood it and I felt the same. Totally the same.

"So much change," she breathed out.

"I know. But you're gonna be the best mom. I can't wait to be a daddy to whatever little love bug comes into our world."

Marnie snuggled into me and we kissed for awhile before going out to the couch to see if any good movies were on. We spontaneously poured cereal, though it was nighttime, and lovingly and dorkily fed each other bites of it. But we didn't get fifteen minutes into the movie before Marnie jumped into my lap, straddling me, and had her mouth pressed to mine like we were the toughest glue on Earth.

Just as great as our honeymoon. Maybe better.

Eighty

Marnie

Monday, May 20th, 2019. 4:41 PM. San Luis Obispo, CA

We upgraded to a two bedroom apartment. I was so thrilled and relieved that Eldon's grocery store job and his freelance work writing skits for schools and churches helped us get what we needed for our soon-to-arrive baby. I helped where I could too. I didn't write as much with my lack of energy and focus, but I managed to tutor kids in English online.

We spent one day lounging and eating on the floor of our second bedroom, the one for the baby, and I had no trouble scarfing down a wacky collision of bacon, mashed potatoes, and a bowl of marshmallow cereal. All in the same sitting.

"What if I start cussing or screaming like a banshee? I don't know how I'm gonna handle the pain."

"You'll be a warrior," Eldon said. He had his back against the wall, legs stretched out in front of him, barefoot in sweatpants, shirtless, and his long hair cascaded down his chest and into his eyes as he leaned over to pick up a marshmallow that had escaped his spoon.

More of a sexy vision now for some reason. I'm so lucky. How did he pick me? How is this real? Oh, El... swoon.

"I hope so," I said.

"I'm with you, my love. I can't wait to meet our baby."

I scooped another bite of mashed potatoes and put it in my mouth. *Hungry, tired, nauseous. Ugh. Hope it gets better.*

Eighty-One

Eldon

Wednesday, August 28th, 2019. 7:02 PM.

The birth of our son... he's here. I'm a dad.

Alone with Marnie in the hospital room for the first time in several hours, I sat close with her as she held baby Halfdan to her chest. I watched both of them breathe peacefully after their long day.

Exhausted. Beautiful. So precious. My precious family.

Seeing Marnie's eyes open and hearing her gentle moan as she shifted to a more comfortable position, I leaned in to whisper, "You have no idea how proud I am of you."

She barely smiled, but she gripped my hand, beckoning me to hold Halfdan again. I took him in my arms, but stayed close to her, touching my forehead to hers. We breathed together, her breath more raspy than mine, and she said in a soft voice, "I love you so much, El."

I wept holding Halfdan, not gonna lie, and I paced around the room with him, whispering the stories of Arrowswan and Jaeger Bowen into his little ears.

Halfdan Eldon Cornade. I love you, little elfling. My son.

Eighty-Two

Eldon

Monday, October 14th, 2019. 1:21 AM. San Luis Obispo, CA

Drafting a new screenplay idea to send to Mark, (since he finally had his own independent film company starting up!), I found myself constantly torn in various directions from being loving husband, patient daddy, and diligent, productive writer.

Marnie was in the middle of trying to get Halfdan back to sleep, and I heard the commotion from our bedroom. I set my reading glasses down and went into the baby's room, seeing Marnie sitting in a pile of shirts she was working on folding with one arm with Halfdan wailing against her, and Marnie herself almost in tears as she struggled to put things in a neat stack.

I didn't question why she was doing it all in the middle of the night. She kept beating herself up about not being a good enough wife and mom and was upset when Halfdan wouldn't stop crying for hours at a time.

The fact that my Elf queen was draped in a baggy sweatshirt and stained pants, covered in drool, snot, and dried poop… that didn't

213

deter me from swooping in to comfort her.

"Let me take him and you get in the bath."

"But you're writing. I know you're busy working on a screenplay for Mark."

"That's okay. Take a bath, love."

Marnie stood up with Halfdan, caught a glimpse of herself in the mirror, and started to cry. "I feel so gross, Eldon! Every room is a mess, crumbs on all the floors and our room, and I can't fit in my sexy clothes. I can't! I feel like throwing up and I'm so hungry. I just wanna lie down for ten hours!"

I put my arms around her, smelling blueberry conditioner in her sweaty, tangled hair. She kept trembling as she sobbed and I touched a hand to her chin, turning her face to look in my eyes. "Hey. Elf queens battle goblin snot and troll drool all the time. You got this, Arrowswan. It's just a temporary season in our kingdom's walls."

"How do you know? I could feel and look gross forever."

"I don't care what you look like. Even if every goblin has spit their mucus and dragons have flung gloppy turds all over you, I'd still call you beautiful."

She shook her head, wiping her nose on her sleeve.

"I'm serious," I said. "I've never been more attracted to you, muffin. You're a sexy warrior mama."

"You're laying it on too thick, El."

"I'm not. And I'm not upset to be pulled away from my writing. You have sacrificed just as much. I know you wish you had more time to write."

"But," Marnie said, handing Halfdan to me, "I can't even think of stories anymore. I feel so foggy and cluttered in my head."

"It'll come back to you. I know it will, Marnie. Now, take a bath. Relax. Turn some Enya on."

She started to leave the room, but then turned and said over her shoulder, "I'm sorry, El."

"For what?"

"For not being able to handle all this."

"You're doing amazing. It's just a rough valley. We'll get through it. We'll get through it with our little elfling."

"Elfling," Marnie echoed with a weary smile at Halfdan. "He is. Lucky he's got an Elf king for a daddy."

I smiled and kissed her cheek. "Go relax. I've got him."

I got you, Danny, I thought as I bounced with Halfdan. *You and your mama are my favorite people in the whole world.*

Eighty-Three

Marnie

Friday, December 6th, 2019. 12:31 AM

Halfdan turned out to be quite a handful the first few months of his life. I knew babies were hard work and kids in general, but the exhaustion of calming my baby boy and trying to hold myself together was always a mental and physical battle. I cried a lot with him.

Eldon surprised me on one of those long nights while I was fighting to get Halfdan back to sleep. He wrapped his arms around my waist, kissed my neck, and held a piece of paper in front of my face. "Read it," he whispered.

Swaying with fussy Halfdan, I did read it. Silently. It was a dorky handwritten "love coupon". Then out loud I said, "What's a spark date?"

"I know you worry about us keeping the spark alive, and even though I love you more than anything, I figured I should prove it."

"And?"

"Tomorrow you and I are dressing up as king and queen Elves and going to an art gallery. We'll pretend like we belong there and talk about it as if we are experts."

I teared up, embarrassed at how sensitive I felt. "That sounds awesome."

"Yeah," Eldon said. "Will you go out with me, my queen?"

"Always," I said.

We kissed in the dark kitchen, giggling at how the floor was sticky with a juice spill from the night before.

* * *

The "spark dates" became a regular thing for us. Thanks to my sweet, sexy, amazing husband. Even when I was having a rough day, Eldon knew how to motivate me. He knew how to make me smile.

* * *

Saturday, December 7th, 2019. 6:03 PM

We dressed up as king and queen Elves and went to an art gallery. I wondered how security would react to us in our layers of clothing that could potentially hide some dangerous object, but they just chuckled at us and let us go about our way. That made me wonder how Eldon handled going through the airport security dressed all in his Jaeger Bowen outfit when he came home from quitting his New York job.

"Oh, that was a little hassle," he said.

"Yeah? Little?"

"Okay, maybe a medium one. I did have to shed my armor to go through the scanners. But, you know, I was surprised no one asked for a selfie with me."

"What?" I laughed as we walked through a space art exhibit. "You weren't shy about pictures?"

"I was SO nervous, baby, but excited. I wanted to wow you."

"You did," I said. "Truly. And what about that long and random conversation we had on the beach?"

"Which one?" he asked, giving me a flirty slap on the butt.

"Vow Of The Silent Kindred. I don't think we did anything that we set out to in regards to that whole thing."

Smiling as he looked up at a vibrant red painting, Eldon said softly, "I don't think it's about what we do. It's what we are."

What we are... wow. I married a true literary poet.

"We are the vow, baby. We embody it. Everything that's weird and quirky and adorably goofy. That is VOTSK." He stopped with me at the bottom of a white staircase and held my face in his hands. "You have brought the brightest, purest light to my world."

I stroked strands of hair out of his eyes. "You're corny, you know that?"

"So are you, Arrowswan," he said and leaned in to kiss my ear and neck.

Goosebumps. All over. "Jaeger," I whispered, kissing him back. His mouth was so perfectly gentle and intense at the same time. *Ooooh.*

* * *

Monday, December 16th, 2019. 3:31 PM

One of our weirdest spark dates was when we pretended to track and spy on each other like how some couples do in espionage movies. We dressed up as a slick businessman and a sassy businesswoman and circled each other inside of a mall while accomplishing real shopping and munching soft pretzels. I was, as usual, drooling from the combination of Eldon's attire, physique, and the sight of his long hair flowing as he did several minutes of a goofy male-model-on-a-catwalk walk in one section of a clothing store. I knew he was taunting me, and within thirty minutes of that spark date, I had him pinned to the floor beneath a row of drinking fountains.

Wink. Wink.

* * *

Thursday, February 13th, 2020. 2:20 PM

Our archery spark date drew a big crowd. We went to an archery range, with little experience, and managed to create an epic cheering section while showing off the old world Elf skills we didn't know we had.

Highlight of that day was both of us looking like fantasy Elf warriors on a movie set and taking at least a dozen selfies with people who thought we were famous actors. And the video clips that went viral. At least we looked super attractive in them. No embarrassing trips or falls that day.

Eldon also publicly made out with me which was the most fun thing ever. Just us in our long, flowing hair, cloaks, armor, boots, bows at our backs as we slobbered all over each other in full daylight.

Best husband ever. Always making me feel like an adored queen.

Eighty-Four

Marnie

Wednesday, October 14th, 2020. 3:21 PM

I had seen Eldon eat ice cream out of a cup so many times. It was normal. But for some reason on that day… Watching him tediously dip his spoon into a cup of cookie dough ice cream and put it in his mouth, then give our one-year-old son a bite of it, and go on and on in the same way: eating and sharing it with our son… The way he looked sitting outside all relaxed with his hair pulled back in a loose braid and a few strands falling into his eyes. *Hot guy. My hot guy. Hot husband and daddy.*

"Hey, El?"

"Yeah?"

"I gotta get you home," I said. "Like now."

"Oh really?" he said back in a teasing voice. He still ate small bites of his ice cream, looking around at the random touristy people walking by us. He was oblivious to the growing passion in me.

Before he could give another bite of ice cream to Halfdan, I leaned forward and put my mouth on the spoon, making direct eye contact with him as he realized what I was thinking.

"You wild thing, Arrowswan. All right. Let's go."

Both of us were very giddy and full of energy later that night. Eldon had so much extra swag…

Eighty-Five

Eldon

Monday, April 5th, 2021. 8:31 AM

I knew what Marnie's books meant to her. I knew that she wanted to keep writing. Storytelling was her passion just as it was mine. She tried penning some children's stories and various short works outside of fantasy, but her mind always came back to *Arrowswan*.

Marnie talked about it at night, pacing around, spouting dialogue from her first, the original *Arrrowswan* novel. I would be sitting up in bed, working on my own manuscripts, and we had to take turns keeping little Halfdan occupied.

Mark and I discussed plans for so many movies.

But…there was only one story I could really imagine lighting up the screen. Only one character worthy of being in the spotlight and having her moment of well-deserved glory.

Still being the bachelor that he was, Mark claimed that he was forever married to movies and trying to make his own massive break. But he helped me out on one special project…

A project that I spent months and months on. Late at night and early in the morning. Whenever I had time to write.

For Marnie, I told myself when I was too tired to go on. *For my Marnie. The absolute, no qualms about it, love of my life.*

Eighty-Six

Marnie

Radio silence for a long while. Laid low and didn't record much of our daily happenings. We just did our thing with our little boy. We kept teaching Halfdan everything we could, reading aloud and re-enacting the characters and soda-out-your-nose funny dialogue. And spark dates continued. Eldon never stopped coming up with little surprises and romantic love notes that he taped up everywhere for me to find.

My heart is so full. I feel like magic.

Eighty-Seven

Marnie

Tuesday, February 14th, 2023. 5:45 PM. San Luis Obispo, CA

Eldon and I had a night in on that Valentine's Day. He insisted on doing the cooking while I read to Halfdan.

"Hey, baby?"

I glanced up to see him coming toward me with a mug of coffee balanced on top of an old school binder. "What's that?"

"I want you to read the title of the screenplay I just finished writing."

"You finished it? When?"

"A couple months ago."

I moved over on the floor so he could sit next to me and little Danny. "I wanna see it," I said with a smile. "But why did you put it in an old binder? I thought you were done using those?"

"Don't you remember? This was the one I had when we met in college."

I took the coffee as Eldon took the book from me and positioned himself so Halfdan could sit in his lap.

"Wow," I said. "It is." I ran my fingers over the binder's cover and looked up at his grin. "What?"

"Look at the title, babe."

I opened to the first page and my hand flew to my mouth. "No! You did?!"

Eldon laughed at my reaction. He let Halfdan wriggle out of his arms and leaned into me, kissing my cheek. "I did, my queen."

I struggled to speak. It was *Arrowswan*. My book *Arrowswan* in script format. I started flipping through it, seeing all that he had kept the same. "You kept the talking animals, El!"

"Yeah. They won me over." He still smiled while I looked amazed and just secretly wanted to make out with him all night under the covers.

"And guess what?" he said.

"What?"

"Mark's already got a copy of it. He said he'll start pitching it to producers with his team."

"Really?" I asked. I couldn't contain my excitement. I didn't know what to do or how to let it out.

"Yes. Absolutely, yes, my love."

Eighty-Eight

Eldon

⁂

10:34 PM

When Halfdan was finally in bed, we turned on *Return Of The King.* We made it fifty minutes in and Marnie was on top of me, pouring out all the intense passion she had apparently stored up over the past several hours.

Epic night, I told myself over and over. *I'm running out of words to describe how amazing this is. How amazing my gorgeous wife is. My life. My love. My treasure.*

My thoughts bumbled around and shut down the second she climbed onto my lap. We just melted into each other.

Every time is the best time, I thought. *Beautiful, precious Marnie.*

Eighty-Nine

Marnie

Monday, August 28th, 2023. 1:15 PM. San Simeon, CA

We were at a glorious beach house for our son's fourth birthday. Just me, El, and little Halfdan. I left the two of them playing in the sand to make some sandwiches in the house and bring them out for an improvised picnic. I could hear Halfdan's excited giggling as he watched Eldon show him the art of making drippy sandcastles, knowing that he was just gonna mess up his daddy's efforts the second it was built. *Rascal.*

My phone rang as soon as I reached the sand again, and I had to shift the bag of food to my other hand as I answered it.

"Marnie," the voice simply said.

"Mark?" I asked. I stopped in my tracks, looking at where Eldon and Halfdan were playing.

"Yeah," Mark said. "Remember how El turned your novel into a screenplay? Well…"

And what he said after that just echoed round and round in my ears. I ran toward Eldon, shrieking as I dropped my phone and the sandwich bag in the sand.

"Eldon! Eldon, Mark called!"

Eldon stood, catching me in his arms, spinning us around as I almost fell over. "What happened? What'd he say?"

"*Arrowswan* is gonna be a real movie! The script! They liked your script and they are gonna make it a movie!"

"Yes!" Eldon yelled. "Your story's gonna be on the screen, baby!"

Halfdan was watching us, totally confused, and I had to pick him up to bring him into the celebration.

"It's gonna be a movie, Danny!" I said, kissing his head as he continued to give us his serious little blue-eyed stare.

"Oh my gosh, Marn," Eldon said. "It's really happening."

"Your screenplay," I said. "I'm proud of you, love. It's your movie too!" I fought to hold back happy tears, but they flowed when Eldon kissed me and picked both me and Halfdan up in the biggest, adrenaline-fueled superhero embrace.

We did this together. All of it.

Ninety

Eldon

1:55 PM

My love for Marnie and Halfdan was so intense in that moment. I loved them to death regardless of what happened, but seeing the joy and hard work pay off meant much more. *Everything I've ever dreamed of is right here in front of me.* I thought that as I embraced them, and I believed it one hundred percent.

The days before had been tremendous and magical. The journey of my life had been an absolute roller coaster. And that moment. That moment when we got the call from Mark. It was perfect. It was a perfect moment. It was happiness. Elation. Relief.

So grateful, I thought. *So grateful to be alive with this beautiful woman as my wife and this precious miracle as my son. I don't even want to use the word lucky. I'm honored. I feel so loved by God and my family. And I know, with everything in my heart, that no matter what comes our way... we can make it. We can keep making it.*

Ninety-One

Marnie

Tuesday, September 12th, 2056. 3:28 PM

I toss the paper airplane across the cabin. It flies straight to Eldon and he deftly catches it in his hand while smiling at me over his typewriter. I smile back, seeing his dimples as he reads what I wrote.

Paper Airplane Message from Marnie: **I thought you'd never ask, my love. I'll always say yes to a walk with you.**

My vibrant red hair is more of a silvery orange now. Eldon's long blond hair has gone grey, making him look more like a retired wizard than a heartthrob Elf prince. But there's nothing but love when we stare at each other from opposite ends of the room.

Our son Halfdan is now fully grown and doing well for himself as an aerospace engineer. He is dating a sweet woman named Heidi who happens to be a high-spirited history buff. It's been fun when those two come around to visit during the holidays and remind us of how starry-eyed we were in our youth.

Unfortunately, my book *Arrowswan* did not end up becoming a movie. Somewhere down the line the whole thing toppled and burned like a renegade wildfire… which I've been told is normal in the film industry. But great things have still happened in our world. Greater than we could have dreamed on our own.

We own a lakefront cabin plus five acres. *YES.* Which is thanks to years of endless patience, prayer, and nine outstanding screenplays that Eldon was able to profit from alongside our good ole filmmaker buddy Mark. We also have eight beautiful dogs which is above and beyond my happiest wishes. We like to line them up on command and tell people their names in a very specific order:

Aspen the male Alaskan Malamute, Herbie the male Beagle, Magic the male Springer Spaniel, Mei the female Border Collie, Shenandoah the male Yellow Labrador, Havlana the female Black Labrador, Skye the female Golden Retriever, and Major the male German Shepherd.

Eldon and I are so in love with all of them. Blessed in a way that can't be explained. Blessed sometimes feels like too simple a word, but we are. We don't ever take a single second of our lives for granted. If we did back in the day, we don't now.

In this world there are happy and sad endings. Bittersweet and terrible endings. Some endings feel unfinished. And some endings may appear like a single period at the end of a long-winded sentence. But I'd say that to have a great love and adventure, it takes all these things mixed together in one. Me and Eldon? Our ending is well-balanced.

We have lived. We have loved. And we continue on. Tomorrow could be better or worse than the last. But I'll always be his Arrowswan. And he'll always be my Jaeger Bowen. Together. Til death do us part.

We look at the water, at our dogs happily racing around us, half of the pack swimming in the lake. We're barefoot on the edge of the dock, soaking in the late afternoon sunshine, the gentle breeze wafting through our hair. Standing behind me with his arms wrapped around my waist, Eldon brushes his lips against my ear and gently whispers,

"We did good, baby."

I turn around to give him a kiss, and he kisses me first, gliding his hands up my back and onto my neck, cupping my chin as he holds his mouth to mine.

We did. We did good.

About the Author

Han M Greenbarg has been in love with writing fiction since childhood. She is an avid coffee drinker, proud dog mom, and lover of country music and war movies. Her biggest jolts of inspiration stem from nature, a variety of film scores, and animals of all kind.

You can connect with me on:

🔗 https://www.instagram.com/hanmgreenbargauthor

Also by Han M Greenbarg

Scurts Flightplan

Revenge is best served warm, so says my associate Robbie Decker. Kill your demons. They won't plague you again. Really. Then how do you explain my current situation? Locked up in the company of airport eccentrics, friend to a pardoned killer, and pacing the million degree terminal with my wine-drunk therapist. Three months left to live…and I think I got blood on my hands. Talk about your midlife crisis. Where did I go wrong?—From The Journal of Damon Scurto

Elf Bat Book One Kiah

Twelve years after the ruthless massacre of his parents and most of his kin, eighteen-year-old Elf Bat Kiah lives a life of internalized grief and solitude in his family's cave. The arrival of Fly, a reckless purebred Elf maiden, sparks the flame for revenge and a resurgence of the Bats.

Elf Bat Book Two Sacrifice

The revenge of the Elf Bats has begun in Sidhovvn, each Bat warrior facing down the count who carried out the ruthless slaughter of their family. But in the midst of seeking justice against the purebred king and his soldiers, the sudden emergence of Fly's demon-driven adoptive mother Ixetmori proves to be the bigger test of wills, and the defining moment of what it means to be courageous.

Chehnuh

Year 2018. Chehnuh, a half-elven and sole survivor of his people's genocide, resides quietly in a remote cabin in the Sierra Nevada mountains. No one knows how he came to the United States. No one knows that he is part Elf. He is a mystery to all who meet him until a young widowed mother interrupts his peaceful life with a baby and the shadow of a deadly stalker, forever changing how Chehnuh sees his own past, humanity, and the heroic role he has yet to play in today's world.

Byrne

Imagination is survival. That's what he tells them. Full of weird quirks and crazy story ideas, novelist Maddox Byrne can't figure out how to connect with normal people. Ever since the lockdown began and the residents of Tower 881 were trapped together, all he's wanted was to keep morale high and finally get the woman of his dreams to notice him. But every person has a breaking point. Every person longs for what they can't have. How long can humanity live in distrust and paranoia? How long before every person loses their mind? Imagination. Imagination is survival. But can it really save us?

Firemartenn

Blamed for his father's death and the doom of Ateinekus, fifteen-year-old Jet must prove his worth as Firemartenn to the village elders. But the fire dragon king won't let just anyone reach the sacred Ackellhnn's sapphire. Jet has to play by Feuskarg's rules in order to save his family and be the hero he's always wanted to be.

Riverduna

Year 2098. Seventeen-year-old Riverduna lives carefree in Nameus, enjoying the peace of the rooftops and her attic books. But loneliness and a desire for adventure draws her toward the Paedors. When she is given the chance to visit Dredgar, her view of both worlds is turned upside down. Can she learn the ways of the streets without losing her Sky heart to darkness?

Champion pit fighter Dunn knows every survival trick on the streets, but he fears for the future of his baby sister and all the children in the city. Violence between district gangs is escalating each day with no end in sight. Can he find a way to change the lawlessness and brutality of Dredgar before more of his loved ones are killed?

When their paths cross, Riverduna and Dunn realize that it's up to them to take on the harrowing journey to discover the truth about their worlds… and to find peace and love in the darkest of places.